AMERICAN VOICES FROM

A Century of Immigration

1820—1924

AMERICAN VOICES FROM

A Century of Immigration
1820—1924

Rebecca Stefoff

 **Marshall Cavendish**
Benchmark
New York

Marshall Cavendish Benchmark
99 White Plains Road
Tarrytown, New York 10591-9001
www.marshallcavendish.us

Library of Congress Cataloging-in-Publication Data
Stefoff, Rebecca, 1951–
A century of immigration : 1820–1924 / by Rebecca Stefoff.
p. cm. — (American voices from)
Summary: "Describes the diverse peoples who came to the United States from 1820, when records began to be kept, to 1924, when the gates were nearly closed to immigrants. The reactions of Americans to the new arrivals, laws that were passed, and the experiences of the immigrants themselves are covered through the use of primary sources"—Provided by publisher.
Includes bibliographical references and index.
ISBN-13: 978-0-7614-2172-6
ISBN-10: 0-7614-2172-6
1. United States—Emigration and immigration—History—Juvenile literature. 2. Immigrants—United States—History—Juvenile literature.
I. Title. II. Series.

JV6450.S84 2007   304.8'73009038—dc22
2005035963

Printed in Malaysia
1 3 5 6 4 2

Editor: Joyce Stanton
Editorial Director: Michelle Bisson
Art Director: Anahid Hamparian
Series design and composition: Anne Scatto / PIXEL PRESS
Photo Research by Linda Sykes Picture Research, Inc., Hilton Head, SC

ON THE COVER: Painted in 1887, in the middle of the century of immigration, this illustration shows immigrant passengers gazing at the towering symbol of the land they hope will be their new home.

ON THE TITLE PAGE: Photography was invented during the century of immigration, making photos such as this one—immigrants arriving around 1905—valuable primary sources. The photographer was Lewis W. Hine, who used his camera to document issues and events in American history, including the abuses of child labor and the construction of the Empire State Building.

Acknowledgments

The author is grateful to Zachary Harris of C/Z Harris Ltd. for his invaluable research services.

Permission has been granted to use quotations from the following copyrighted works:

Extract from "Catherine Moran McNamara" from *First Generation: In the Words of Twentieth-Century American Immigrants.* Copyright 1978, 1992 by June Namias. Used with permission of the University of Illinois Press.

Extract from *Through Harsh Winters: The Life of a Japanese Immigrant Woman* by Akemi Kikumura. Used with permission of Chandler & Sharp Publishers, Inc.

"Poem by One Named Xu," from *Island: Poetry and History of Chinese Immigrants on Angel Island, 1910–1940* by Hiam Mark Lai, Genny Lim, and Judy Yung, published by the Chinese Culture Foundation, 1980. Reprinted by permission of the University of Washington Press.

Extract from *Quiet Odyssey: A Pioneer Korean Woman in America* by Mary Paik Lee, published by the University of Washington Press, 1990. Reprinted by permission of the University of Washington Press.

Extract from *Barrio Boy* by Ernesto Galarza. Copyright 1971 by University of Notre Dame Press, South Bend, Indiana 46556.

"Song of the Exile," from *How Shall We Sing in a Foreign Land? Music of Irish Catholic Immigrants in the Antebellum United States,* copyright 1996 by University of Notre Dame Press, South Bend, Indiana 46556.

Extract from letter by Joseph Hollingsworth from *Witnessing America* by Noel Rae, copyright 1996 by Noel Rae and The Stonesong Press, Inc., pp. 41–42.

Extract from *A Frontier Family in Minnesota: Letters of Theodore and Sophie Bost, 1851–1920,* published by the University of Minnesota Press, 1981. Used with permission of the University of Minnesota Press.

Contents

About Primary Sources   ix

Introduction: Coming to America   xv

Chapter 1 | Law and Policy   1

The First Immigration Law: The Naturalization Act of 1790   4
1882: The Chinese Exclusion Act Shuts the Door   5
"A Proper Immigration Law": Theodore Roosevelt's Message to Congress, 1901   8
By the Numbers: The Johnson-Reed Act of 1924   10

Chapter 2 | American Attitudes toward the Newcomers   14

Nativists Present Their Policies   18
Against Nativism: A Physician Speaks Out   20
"Their Touch Is Pollution": Bayard Taylor's Views on the Chinese   22
A Senator from Massachusetts Condemns the Chinese Exclusion Act   24
"Let Us Shut the Door": Fears of Race Suicide   26
Prejudice: "The Crux of the Immigration Question"   29

Chapter 3 | From All the World   33

"America as We Imagine It": A Swiss Immigrant's Letter Home   35
Promises to Chinese Emigrants: "All Is Nice"   37
From Dalmatia: John Tadich Crosses the Plains   39
The Melting-Pot: Israel Zangwill Coins a Powerful Phrase   41
Jacob Riis Casts an "Unblinking Eye at the Motley Crowd"   43

Chapter 4 | Leaving Home   46

A Chinese Boy Hears of the "American Wizards"   49
"Oleana": A Dream Becomes a Disaster   50
Talking and Going Are Two Different Things: Notes from a Welshman   52
Immigrants Helping Emigrants: "I Wish I Could Go with You"   54
An Irish Family on the Move   55
From Korea to Hawaii in 1905   57

Chapter 5 | *Passages and Arrivals*   *61*

    A Voice from the Steerage   64

    "The Ship Was Our World": Mary Antin Crosses the Atlantic   66

    "Unfortunate Travellers": A Chinese Immigrant's Poem of
       Consolation   68

    Evelyn Berkowitz: A Passage from Hungary   70

    A Greek Immigrant Remembers Ellis Island   71

Chapter 6 | *Life in the New Country*   *74*

    Enjoying Equality: A Former Englishman Writes Home   77

    Mother Jones: An Immigrant Woman and the Labor Movement   78

    Missing the Homeland: The Irish "Song of the Exile"   80

    A Norwegian Settler Writes from the Frontier   83

    "Liberty Only through Force": George Engel of the Chicago Eight   85

    Golden Dreams, Ragged Reality: Rocco Corresca Remembers
       His *Padrone*   88

    A Danish Immigrant's *American Saga*   90

Chapter 7 | *Becoming American*   *93*

    The First German-American Senator: Carl Schurz Enters Politics   95

    "Be Worthy": Advice for Immigrants   98

    A Bulgarian Immigrant Makes a Decision   99

    Ernesto Galarza: "The Americanization of Mexican Me"   101

    A Note on the Principle of "Americanization"   102

    Preserving the Immigrant Heritage: Akemi Kikumura   103

    Time Line   *106*

    Glossary   *110*

    To Find Out More   *111*

    Index   *113*

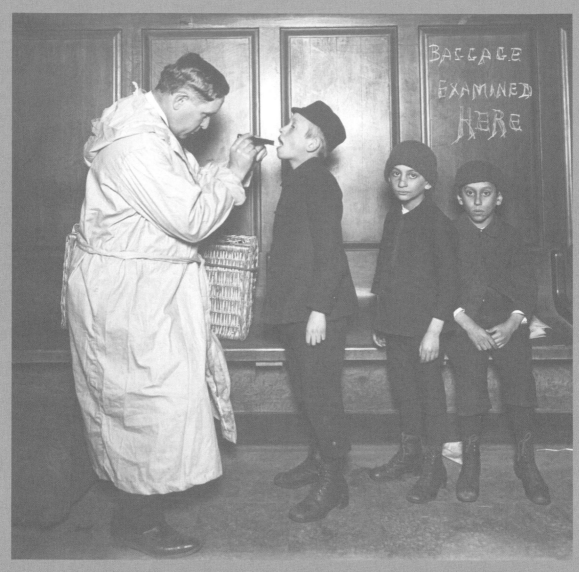

A city health officer examines immigrant children in New York City in 1911, when people feared that newcomers were carrying the deadly disease typhus into the city. Easily spread in unsanitary conditions, typhus was one of the illnesses that raged on some immigrant vessels.

About Primary Sources

What Is a Primary Source?

In the pages that follow, you will be hearing many different "voices" from a special time in America's past. Some of the selections are long and others are short. You'll find many easy to understand at first reading, while others may require several readings. All the selections have one thing in common, however. They are primary sources. That is the name historians give to the bits and pieces of information that make up the record of human existence. Primary sources are important to us because they are the core material of all historical investigation. You might call them "history" itself.

Primary sources are evidence; they give historians the all-important clues they need to understand the past. Perhaps you have read a detective story in which a sleuth must solve a mystery by piecing together bits of evidence he or she uncovers. The detective makes deductions, or educated guesses based on the evidence, and solves the mystery once all the deductions point in a certain direction. Historians work in much the same way. Like detectives, historians analyze data through careful reading and rereading.

New arrivals pack the benches in the main hall of the U.S. Immigration Station on Ellis Island in the early 1900s. Waiting to be formally admitted to the United States was an anxious time for the immigrants, who ran the risk of being denied entrance and forced to return home.

After much analysis, historians draw conclusions about an event, a person, or an entire era. Individual historians may analyze the same evidence and come to different conclusions. That is why there is often sharp disagreement about an event.

Primary sources are also called documents. This rather dry word can be used to describe many different things: an official speech by a government leader, an old map, an act of Congress, a letter worn out from much handling, an entry hastily scrawled in a diary, a detailed newspaper account of an event, a funny or sad song, a colorful poster, a cartoon, an old painting, a faded photograph, or someone's remembrances captured on tape or film.

By examining the following documents, you the reader will be taking on the role of historian. Here is your chance to immerse yourself in a movement that forever changed the United States: the great wave of immigration that swept into the country between 1820 and 1924. This century of immigration brought millions of new citizens to America. They came from dozens of countries around the world, bringing languages, beliefs, customs, and memories that in time became part of America's shared cultural landscape. Many of these immigrants recorded their experiences and thoughts. You'll hear from men, women, and children who made long, difficult journeys to America, and you'll discover what they found when they arrived. You'll also hear from the Americans who welcomed immigrants and from those who feared them—from lawmakers, journalists, and ordinary citizens on both sides of the great immigration debate.

Our language has

The dining hall on Ellis Island. Located in New York Harbor, Ellis Island was the point of entry for most people coming to start new lives in the United States.

changed since the nineteenth and early twentieth centuries. Some words and expressions will be unfamiliar to a person living in the early twenty-first century. Even familiar words may have been spelled differently then. In addition, some of the primary sources in this book were written by people who were still learning English (others have been translated from the immigrants' native languages). Don't be discouraged! Trying to figure out language is exactly the kind of work a historian does. Like a historian, you will end with a deeper, more meaningful understanding of the past.

How to Read a Primary Source

Each document in this book deals with some aspect of immigration between 1820 and 1924. Some of the documents are part of public or official history, such as immigration laws, a presidential speech, and a scene from a famous play. Others are drawn from the lives of ordinary people, such as letters immigrants wrote to the families they left behind and recollections—sometimes after many years—of their journeys to America and their first experiences there. All of these documents help us understand what it was like to live during the century of immigration.

As you read each document, ask yourself some basic questions. Who is writing or speaking? Who is that person's audience? What is the writer's point of view? What is he or she trying to tell the audience? Is the message clearly expressed, or is it implied, that is, stated indirectly? What words does the writer use to convey his or her message? Are the words emotional or objective in tone? If you are looking at a newspaper cartoon, a photograph, or another work of art, examine it carefully, taking in all the details. What is happening in the foreground? In the background? What is its purpose? These are questions that can help you think critically about a primary source.

Some tools have been included with the documents to help you in your investigations. Unusual words have been listed and defined near the selections, and thought-provoking questions follow them. They help focus your reading so you can get the most out of each document. As you read each selection, you'll probably come up with many questions of your own. That's great! The work of a historian always leads to many, many questions. Some can be answered, while others require more investigation. Perhaps when you finish this book, your questions will lead you to further explorations of the century of immigration.

A pretzel vendor in New York's Lower East Side, 1900. Cheap housing made that part of the city home to many newly arrived immigrants.

Jewish immigrants enter New York Harbor in this illustration, made in 1892. That year the Ellis Island immigration station opened in the harbor. It would be the starting point for millions of immigrants for the next fifty years.

Introduction

COMING TO AMERICA

"And then," said Estelle Schwartz Belford, "all of a sudden we heard a big commotion and we came to America and everybody started yelling they see the Lady, the Statue of Liberty, and we all ran upstairs and everybody started screaming and crying. We were kissing each other. . . . Everybody was so excited that you see America and see the Lady with her hand up, you know." Belford was describing how she and her family had arrived in the United States thirty-six years earlier, in 1905, when she was five years old. They had come from Romania in eastern Europe, and when they saw the Statue of Liberty rising above the harbor of New York City, they knew an extraordinary moment had come.

The people cheering and kissing on that ship were part of a long American tradition of immigration, one that continues today. Everyone who lives in the Americas came from someplace else, or is descended from people who came from someplace else. Even the Native Americans, the Indian peoples who were the first inhabitants of the Americas, came from Asia thousands of years ago. When we talk about immigration, though, we aren't usually referring to ancient migrations—we're talking about people who have come voluntarily to the United States from around the world in recent historical times. No one knows their exact number, but it is many, many millions. The U.S. government began keeping records of immigrant arrivals at American seaports in 1820. A little more than a hundred years later, in 1924, a new federal law sharply limited the number of immigrants who could enter the country. During the century of immigration between those two events, 40

Pushcart vendors in Little Italy, a part of New York's Manhattan borough where many Italian immigrants lived and worked. Primary sources such as this 1897 photograph document not just immigrant history but also the growth of New York and other American cities.

million immigrants are known to have entered the United States, according to the *Statistical Yearbook* of the federal Bureau of Citizenship and Immigration Services. Young Estelle and her family from Romania were part of the immense human tide that swept onto American shores during the century of immigration, reshaping society and changing millions of lives.

Immigration before 1820 is not very well documented. Historians have had to piece together an account of it by drawing on many primary sources, including letters and diaries, population counts of cities and towns, lists of ships' passengers, and the sketchy and incomplete records of the British North American colonies and later of the states. These sources reveal that in 1775, when the American colonies began their fight for independence from Great Britain, the colonies' total population was highly diverse. Nearly one-fifth of the population was black, although enslaved Africans are not usually called immigrants because they

A merchant offers his wares in San Francisco's Chinatown, 1890. This lively ethnic neighborhood still thrives today.

came to America involuntarily, brought by force. The colonial population also included people from nearly every part of Europe as well as a few Pacific Islanders and Asians. But the largest national group among the colonists was English. Together with others from the British Isles—the Scottish, Irish, Scots-Irish, and Welsh colonists—they dominated the ethnic makeup of the Thirteen Colonies. Germans formed the largest non-British group, followed by the Dutch, Swedes, and French.

Once the United States had gained its independence, it had to decide what to do about immigration. From the start, Americans held two opposing views on the subject. The inclusive or open view welcomed a wide range of newcomers and placed few barriers in their way. Perhaps some of those who held this view were immigrants, or remembered that their parents or grandparents had been immigrants. Others felt that the new nation needed the labor and energy of immigrants to tame its wildernesses, build its cities, work in its shops and factories, and people its enormous landscapes. Still others held religious or political principles of equality that made them feel that America should be open to all. Among these was Jonathan Trumbull, governor of Connecticut, who wrote in a 1782 letter:

> Our interests and our laws teach us to receive strangers, from every quarter of the globe, with open arms. The poor, the unfortunate, the oppressed from every country, will find here a ready asylum;—and by uniting their interests with ours, enjoy in common with us, all the blessings of liberty and plenty. Neither difference of nation, of language, of

manners, or of religion, will lessen the cordiality of their reception among a people whose religion teaches them to regard all mankind as their brethren.

Although George Washington, the new nation's first president, sometimes expressed concerns about immigrants' loyalty, for the most part he held the open view. Washington once told some immigrants newly arrived from Ireland, "The Bosom of America is open to receive not only the Opulent [wealthy] and respectable Stranger but the oppressed and persecuted of all Nations and Religions." But his fellow founding fathers Benjamin Franklin and Thomas Jefferson feared that large numbers of non-English foreigners in the country, speaking their own languages, following their own customs, and living in their own communities,

Many people left their homelands to escape ethnic and religious persecution, such as this anti-Semitic riot in Moravia (now part of the Czech Republic).

would threaten national unity. They held the exclusive or closed view of immigration, which saw a need to limit and control entry into the country, to admit only "desirable" foreigners. That view was shared by John Jay, the first chief justice of the U.S. Supreme Court, who wrote in 1787 that the United States was and should remain "one united people—a people descended from the same ancestors, speaking the same language, professing the same religion, attached to the same principles of government." During America's first century of mass immigration, from 1820 to 1924, conflicting ideas about immigration shaped the laws and public policies that determined who could enter the United States—and what kind of receptions they would find.

But the views of Americans are only half of the story of immigration. Equally vital are the motives, thoughts, and experiences of the emigrants who left their homelands to come to the United States. People emigrated for many reasons. Many who came during the century of immigration, like many who had come to the American colonies in the seventeenth and eighteenth centuries, were driven by economic factors. Quite simply, they wanted a better life for themselves and their children than they could have in their homelands, and they believed they could find it in America. That dream often took the form of owning land. In some countries, such as Norway, there was simply no more farmland available. In others, such as England, prosperous landowners owned or were buying up all the land, reducing peasant farmers to tenants or hired laborers. Some emigrants hoped to earn better wages in America's growing cities than they could earn at home. Others were lured by tales of the country's rich natural resources, from waters teeming with fish

to soil so rich it barely needed to be tilled to western mountains full of gold.

A better, safer, and more prosperous life for their children was the goal of many immigrants.

Emigrants also came to the United States in search of political or religious freedom. Many Europeans yearned to live in a democracy, especially after the failure of widespread revolutionary movements that had tried to bring democracy to Europe in the 1840s. Others, such as the Jews who left eastern Europe and Russia, wanted to escape religious or ethnic persecution. Many people emigrated for more than one reason, or simply because they felt that they would have a brighter future in the new country across the sea. Some emigrants were pulled to America, drawn by dreams of improved fortunes or new freedoms. Others were pushed out of their homelands by hostile

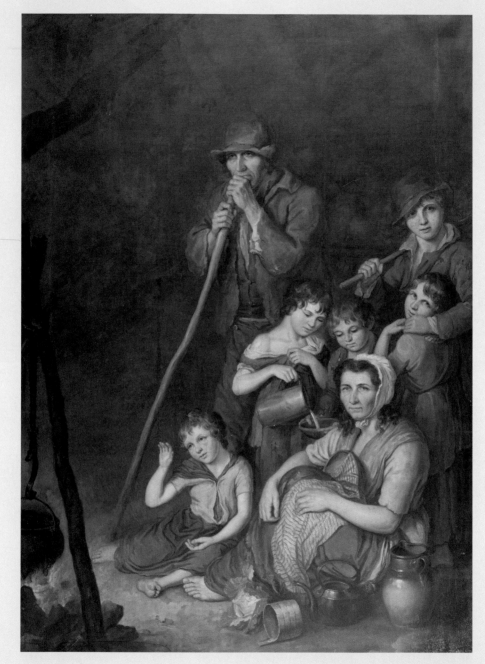

Nineteenth-century painter John Joseph Barker portrayed an Irish family preparing to leave their country. Poverty and starvation drove many Irish to emigrate.

circumstances. A plant disease destroyed Ireland's potato crop between 1845 and 1849, for example, dooming many Irish to starvation and causing thousands more to emigrate. The Taiping Rebellion that began in southern China in the 1850s brought chaos and desperate poverty—turbulent conditions that drove many Chinese to emigrate to California.

Whether they were irresistibly pulled to the glorious vision of America or reluctantly driven from their native countries, all of the immigrants who entered the United States faced the challenges of leaving home, making a long and generally uncomfortable journey, and then establishing themselves in a new, strange land. Those events left their mark on all of them, although each experienced the challenges in a unique way. Fortunately, many immigrants recorded at least part of their experience in the form of letters, journals, or memoirs. Other immigrants' stories were gathered, sometimes decades later, by historians. These valuable primary sources are part of the nation's history and part of the shared history of each ethnic group in American society. They are also human adventures: touching, inspiring, sorrowful, and always individual.

Each immigrant has his or her own story, triumphant or tragic. These stories tell of hard work, victories, and humiliations. Above all they tell of the constant challenge of adjusting old ways and expectations to the sometimes surprising realities of life in America. Many immigrants would probably agree with Gjert G. Hovland, who in 1838 wrote from Illinois to a friend in his native Norway, "I am glad that I came here, although everything has not always gone according to my wishes."

The Last of England, an 1860 painting by British artist Ford Madox Brown, reflects the mood of sorrow that gripped many emigrants as they said farewell to their native shores and set sail for an uncertain future. English immigrants, however, were welcomed in the United States, and they would find it far easier than many others to adapt to life there.

Chapter I

Law and Policy

EFORE THE AMERICAN REVOLUTION, each colony had some ability to set its own standards and rules for immigration and also for naturalization, the process by which an immigrant becomes a citizen in the eyes of the law. Some colonies passed laws designed to prevent criminals or the very poor from settling in them, or to admit only members of particular religions. The government of Great Britain, however, ruled the colonies and could make laws that applied to all of them. It did so with the Naturalization Act of 1740, under which immigrants who had come to the colonies from anywhere in Europe could become British citizens after they had lived in the colonies for seven years. In 1774, as unrest among the colonists rose toward fever pitch, Great Britain outlawed all immigration to the colonies.

In 1790, the newly independent United States passed its first national immigration law. The law didn't limit immigration, but it did specify that only certain immigrants could become U.S. citizens. The decades that followed brought a series of immigration laws. Some of these laws changed the terms under which immigrants could become naturalized citizens. Others tried to control the conditions under which immigrants traveled. For example, the Steerage Act of 1819 said that each immigrant aboard a ship must have a certain amount of space, food, and water. On one hand, this act could have protected immigrants by improving shipboard conditions, which were often dreadful. On the other hand, by reducing crowding, the act could also have reduced the total number of immigrants. In the end it didn't matter—it and other steerage acts, both American and British, were almost never enforced.

Most immigration laws sought to limit immigration into the United States by excluding, or keeping out, certain kinds of people. The categories of people who were excluded changed over time, reflecting the changing fears of the American public and its lawmakers. After the first large-scale immigration by Asians—Chinese workers who began arriving in California in the mid-nineteenth century—prejudice led to a cluster of laws against Chinese immigration. Other laws later banned immigration from Japan, India, and many other parts of Asia. An 1882 law said that criminals, paupers, and insane people could not enter the country. In 1891, when the U.S. government was in conflict with the Mormon territory of Utah, where Mormon law allowed men to have more than one wife, Congress outlawed the immigration of polygamists, or men with multiple wives. Twelve years later, after political extremists called anarchists had carried out assassinations and acts of violence in the United States and other countries, a new U.S. immigration law excluded anarchists from entering; later laws were also aimed at keeping anarchists and others the government viewed as potential troublemakers out of the country. The 1917 Immigration Act set a literacy test. Only immigrants who could read were allowed to enter—but they could read any language, not just English.

The immigration law of 1924 took a different approach. It set a numerical limit on the total number of immigrants who could enter the country each year, and it also set a quota, or specific limit, for immigration from each nation. A similar "quota law" had passed three years earlier, but the 1924 law was stricter. Its effect was immediate and dramatic. Total immigration into the United States in 1924 was 709,896. The following year, after the new law took effect, it dropped to 294,314. The first century of mass immigration was over.

A 1908 illustration from a French newspaper shows a mob attacking an Asian-owned shop in San Francisco. Prejudice against Asian immigrants fueled outbreaks of violence, mostly in the West, where immigrants from China, Japan, Korea, India, and other Asian countries were concentrated.

The story of American immigration had not ended, however. During the 1940s, when the United States was embroiled in World War II, immigration laws began to loosen slightly. The Immigration Reform Act of 1965, which ended the national-origins systems of quotas, launched a new, much more open era in American immigration. Since 1965, immigrants from all parts of the world have been able to enter the United States in much greater numbers than between 1924 and 1965.

The First Immigration Law: The Naturalization Act of 1790

On March 26, 1790, the United States Congress passed the country's first national immigration law. Strictly speaking, it was a naturalization law rather than an immigration law. It did not spell out who could enter the United States, but it did define who could become a U.S. citizen.

SECTION 1

Be it enacted by the Senate and House of Representatives of the United States of America in Congress assembled, That any alien, being a free white person, who shall have resided within the limits and under the jurisdiction of the United States for the term of two years, may be admitted to become a citizen thereof, on application to any common law court of record, in any one of the states wherein he shall have resided for the term of one year at least, and making proof to the satisfaction of such court, that he is a person of good character, and taking the oath or affirmation prescribed by law, to support the constitution of the United States, which oath or affirmation such court shall administer; and the clerk of such court shall record such application, and the proceedings thereon; and thereupon such person shall be considered as a citizen of the United States. And the children of such persons so naturalized, dwelling within the United States, being under the age of twenty-one years at the time of such naturalization, shall also be considered as citizens of the United States. And the children of citizens of the United States that may be born beyond sea, or out of the limits of the United States, shall be considered as natural born citizens: *Provided,* That the right of citizenship shall not descend to persons whose fathers have never been resident in the United States: *Provided also,* That no person heretofore proscribed by any state, shall be admitted a citizen as aforesaid, except by an act of the legislature of the state in which such person was proscribed.

proscribed
banned,
outlawed

—*Reprinted in Dennis Wepman,* Immigration: From the Founding of Virginia to the Closing of Ellis Island, *New York: Facts On File, 2002.*

THINK ABOUT THIS:

1. Who was allowed to become a citizen under the act? Who was not allowed?
2. Does the language of the act make it clear whether women could become naturalized citizens?

1882: The Chinese Exclusion Act Shuts the Door

During the 1870s Americans became increasingly concerned about the growing number of immigrants from China. Some U.S. citizens

Members of the Workingmen's Party demonstrate against Chinese immigration outside San Francisco's city hall in 1879. Protesters' signs bear messages such as "No Chinese Cheap Labor for Us."

resented the fact that Chinese immigrants competed with other laborers for jobs—and were often hired because, desperate to earn a better living than they could make in China, they were willing to work for lower wages than others in the labor market. Other critics simply feared that Asian immigrants would weaken or undermine America's identity, which they saw as white, Christian, and of European descent. Feelings against Chinese immigrants were especially strong in California and other western states, where most of the Asian newcomers had landed. Anti-Chinese riots raged in some western cities. In 1882 Congress responded by passing a law that banned immigration from China for ten years.

WHEREAS, IN THE OPINION OF THE GOVERNMENT of the United States the coming of Chinese laborers to this country endangers the good order of certain localities within the territory thereof: Therefore,

Be it enacted by the Senate and House of Representatives of the United States of America in Congress assembled, That from and after the expiration of ninety days next after the passage of this act, and until the expiration of ten years after the passage of this act, the coming of Chinese laborers to the United States be, and the same is hereby, suspended; and during such suspension it shall not be lawful for any Chinese laborer to come, or, having so come after the expiration of said ninety days, to remain within the United States.

SECTION 2
That the master of any vessel who shall knowingly bring within the United States on such vessel, and land or permit to be landed, any Chinese laborer, from any foreign port or place, shall be deemed guilty of a misdemeanor, and on conviction thereof shall be punished by a fine of not more than five hundreds dollars for each and every such Chinese laborer so brought, and may also be imprisoned for a term not exceeding one year. . . .

". . . no State court or court of the United States shall admit Chinese to citizenship."

SECTION 14
That hereafter no State court or court of the United States shall admit Chinese to citizenship; and all laws in conflict with this act are hereby repealed.

. . . That the words "Chinese laborers," whenever used in this act, shall be constructed to mean both skilled and unskilled laborers and Chinese employed in mining.

—*Reprinted in Dennis Wepman,* Immigration: From the Founding of Virginia to the Closing of Ellis Island, *New York: Facts On File, 2002.*

THINK ABOUT THIS:

1. What freedoms did the Chinese Exclusion Act take away from Chinese people?
2. Does the act include any mechanisms to discourage Chinese immigration? If so, what are they?
3. Do you think Congress acted properly in forbidding the immigration of a specific ethnic group?

"A Proper Immigration Law": Theodore Roosevelt's Message to Congress, 1901

Many Americans were in favor of immigration—as long as only the right *kinds* of immigrants were allowed to enter the country. On May 3, 1901, in his annual message to Congress, President Theodore Roosevelt expressed this view, arguing that the United States needed to keep out poor, ignorant, and immoral immigrants, as well as those he considered politically dangerous.

FIRST, WE SHOULD AIM TO EXCLUDE absolutely not only all persons who are known to be believers in anarchistic principles or members of

Theodore Roosevelt, president from 1901 to 1909, wanted stricter immigration laws, in part to protect the country from potential political troublemakers.

anarchistic societies, but also all persons who are of a low moral tendency or unsavory reputation. . . . The second object of a proper immigration law ought to be to secure by a careful and not merely perfunctory educational test some intelligent capacity to appreciate American institutions and act sanely as American citizens. . . . Finally,

anarchistic
relating to anarchy, a political philosophy that opposes all forms of organized government

all persons should be excluded who are below a certain standard of economic fitness to enter our industrial field as competitors with American labor. There should be a proper proof of personal capacity to earn an American living and enough money to insure a decent start under American conditions. This would stop the influx of cheap labor, and the resulting competition which gives rise to so much of bitterness in American industrial life, and it would dry up the springs of the pestilential social conditions in our great cities, where anarchistic organizations have their greatest possibility of growth.

Both the educational and the economic tests in a wise immigration law should be designed to protect and elevate the general body politic and social.

—*Reprinted in Dennis Wepman,* Immigration: From the Founding of Virginia to the Closing of Ellis Island, *New York: Facts On File, 2002.*

THINK ABOUT THIS:

1. What kinds of tests did Roosevelt want to see applied to would-be immigrants?
2. Would these tests have favored some ethnic groups over others?
3. Do you think Roosevelt's proposals were fair?

By the Numbers: The Johnson-Reed Act of 1924

In 1924 Congress passed the Johnson-Reed Act, sometimes called the Immigration Act of 1924. This law drastically limited the number of immigrants allowed to enter the country each year. It cut total immigration by more than 50 percent, from more than 700,000 people to fewer than 300,000—to be reduced further to 150,000 in 1927. The act also introduced a new and complicated system of national quotas. Each country was given a quota, the maximum number of immigrants from that country who could enter the United States each year. The quotas reflected the existing U.S. population. The number who could immigrate from each country was based on the number of people of that national back-

In 1920, Japanese children wait at Angel Island, the immigration station in San Francisco Bay, to enter the United States. Four years later, a new immigration law would drastically limit the number of people allowed to enter the United States from Asia and many other parts of the world.

ground already in the United States, with a minimum quota of one hundred. The nearby nations of Canada and Mexico, along with the countries of Central and South America, were not included in the quota system because the U.S. government feared angering its neighbors by limiting immigration from them. As far as the rest of the world went, however, the purpose of the new act was clear. Because the existing U.S. population was largely of British, German, and Scandinavian ancestry, the act allowed far more immigrants from northern and western Europe than from southern and eastern Europe, and it allowed only a trickle from Asia, Africa, and the Pacific.

SECTION 11

(a) The annual numerical quota of any nationality shall be 2 per centum of the number of foreign-born individuals of such nationality resident in continental United States as determined by the United States census of 1890, but the minimum quota of any nationality shall be 100.

". . . the minimum quota of any nationality shall be 100."

(b) The annual quota of any nationality for the fiscal year beginning July 1, 1927, and for each fiscal year thereafter, shall be a number which bears the same ratio to 150,000 as the number of inhabitants in continental United States in 1920 having that national origin . . . bears to the number of inhabitants in continental United States in 1920, but the minimum quota of any nationality shall be 100.

(c) For the purpose of subdivision (b) national origin shall be ascertained by determining as nearly as may be . . . the number of inhabitants in the continental United States in 1920 whose origin by birth or ancestry is attributable to such geographic area. Such determination shall not be made by tracing the ancestors or descendants of particular individuals, but shall be based upon statistics of immigration and emigration, together with rates of increase of population . . . and such other data as may be found to be reliable.

—*Reprinted in Dennis Wepman,* Immigration: From the Founding of Virginia to the Closing of Ellis Island, *New York: Facts On File, 2002.*

THINK ABOUT THIS:

What kind of message about the United States did the Johnson-Reed Act send to the other nations of the world?

Chapter 2

American Attitudes toward the Newcomers

I N 1986, THE ONE-HUNDREDTH ANNIVERSARY of the dedication of the Statue of Liberty, New York governor Mario Cuomo described in *New York* magazine what the statue had meant to his mother when she arrived in the United States as an immigrant. "My mother came here by ship from Italy," he said, "and her first glimpse of this great country was when she sighted the Lady of Opportunity, steadfastly lifting her torch. My mother understood immediately the meaning of that beautiful symbol. . . . Lady Liberty said, 'Welcome. You are welcome, and the culture you bring with you is welcome, to blend with all the others into this beautiful mosaic that is America.'"

The Statue of Liberty, which stands on a small island in New York Harbor, was a gift from France to celebrate the founding of the United States. From the start, it was a symbol not just of America but of immigration to America. A plaque fastened to the statue's base was inscribed with the words of "The New Colossus," a poem Emma Lazarus had written in 1883 that compared Lady Liberty with the Colossus of Rhodes, a giant statue said to have straddled the harbor

Two young immigrants from Italy on the voyage to the United States. Taken in 1919, this photograph is a primary source from the final years of the century of mass immigration. It captures the excitement felt by children and young people who saw the journey, with all its discomforts, as an adventure.

of the Greek island of Rhodes in ancient times. Lazarus identified the Statue of Liberty as the "Mother of Exiles" who raises a light of "world-wide welcome." She says to the Old World beyond the ocean:

> Give me your tired, your poor,
> Your huddled masses yearning to breathe free,
> The wretched refuse of your teeming shore.
> Send these, the homeless, tempest-tost to me,
> I lift my lamp beside the golden door!

The Museum of the City of New York houses this manuscript of Emma Lazarus's 1883 poem "The New Colossus," whose words are engraved on the base of the Statue of Liberty.

Although the poem presents an image of immigrants that some people now regard as limited or biased, it reveals an America that saw itself as a welcoming new home for people from around the world.

But a poem written one year earlier shows another view. Thomas Bailey Aldrich, editor of a widely read magazine called the *Atlantic Monthly,* published "Unguarded Gates" in the magazine in 1882. It warned that the nation's open immigration policy was letting "a wild motley throng" rush into the United States, "bringing with them unknown gods and rites," "tiger passions," and "strange tongues" that spoke in "accents of menace alien to our ears." The poem asks, "O Liberty, white Goddess! Is it well / To leave the gates unguarded?" The gates had already begun to close—Congress passed the Chinese Exclusion Act the year Aldrich's poem appeared.

Fears about immigrants grew during the 1890s, which brought a great increase in immigration from southern and eastern Europe

The Statue of Liberty, a gift from France to the United States, instantly became the center of attraction in New York Harbor. Soon it was recognized around the world as a symbol of America.

and parts of Asia. The newcomers included Catholics and Jews, as well as people whose languages weren't related to English or German and people who were nonwhite. Many Protestant Americans of British or northern European descent found these foreigners much more *foreign* than the earlier immigrants. Some began to fear that the immigrants would eventually overwhelm the society they knew and change it beyond recognition, either by simply outnumbering "regular" Americans or by intermarrying and interbreeding with them. The idea that Americans of northern European descent might one day be outnumbered or intermingled with other kinds of people because of immigration came to be called "race suicide." It was a powerful fear of many of those who spoke out against immigration in the late nineteenth and early twentieth centuries.

Tension between Lazarus's and Aldrich's views of immigration, between the open arms of welcome and the closed gates of rejection, has been part of American society since the founding of the country. It continues into the twenty-first century as citizens and politicians weigh issues of security, national identity, the economic costs and benefits of immigrants, and the question of how to deal with illegal immigration.

Nativists Present Their Policies

In the mid-1840s nativists found a voice in the Native American Party, an anti-immigrant political organization that warned of the dangers of unlimited immigration and opposed giving naturalized citizens the right to vote. Although the party won some local elections in eastern states, it soon faded from the political scene. Its ideas did not disappear, however. A decade later a new nativist group arose, the American or Know-Nothing Party. In spite of the difference in names, its views were much like those that follow here, as spelled out by the earlier Native American Party in 1845.

IT IS AN INCONTROVERTIBLE TRUTH that the civil institutions of the United States of America have been seriously affected, and that they now stand in imminent peril from the rapid and enormous increase of the body of residents of foreign birth, imbued with foreign feelings, and of an ignorant and immoral character, who receive, under the present lax and unreasonable laws of naturalization, the elective franchise and the right of eligibility to political office.

. . . The mass of foreign voters, formerly lost among the Natives of the soil, has increased from the ratio of 1 in 40 to 1 in 7! A like advance in fifteen years will leave the Native citizens a minority in their own land! Thirty years ago these strangers came by units and tens—now they swarm by thousands.

"The mass of foreign voters . . . has increased from the ratio of 1 in 40 to 1 in 7!"

. . . The body of adopted citizens, with foreign interests and prejudices, is annually advancing with rapid strides, in geometrical progression. Already it has acquired a control over our elections which cannot be entirely corrected, even by the wisest legislation, until the present generation shall be numbered with the past. Already it has notoriously swayed the course of national legislation, and invaded the purity of local justice. In a few years its unchecked progress would cause it to outnumber the native defenders of our rights, and would then inevitably dispossess our offspring, and its own, of the inheritance for which our fathers bled, or plunge this land of happiness and peace into the horrors of civil war.

—From Address of the Delegates of the Native American National Convention, Assembled at Philadelphia, July 4, 1845, to the Citizens of the United States. *Reprinted in William Dudley, series editor,* Opposing Viewpoints in American History, *vol. 1, San Diego: Greenhaven Press, 1996.*

Think about This:

1. Do any words or phrases in this statement make an especially strong emotional impact, either positive or negative? If so, which ones?

2. What specific threat do immigrants pose to the United States, according to this statement? Do you agree?

Against Nativism: A Physician Speaks Out

In the same year that the Native American party met in Philadelphia and issued its warnings against immigration and naturalization, a physician and writer named Thomas L. Nichols stood before an audience in New York City and delivered a lecture in favor of immigration. The lecture was later published. In it, Nichols argued that immigrants were not harmful to the United States. He went further, claiming that it was America's destiny to bring about "the greatest intermingling of races" and that people have a right to move freely between nations.

THE RIGHT OF MAN TO EMIGRATE from one country to another, is one which belongs to him by his own constitution and by every principle of justice. It is one which no law can alter, and no authority destroy.

. . . Emigration from various countries in Europe to America, producing a mixture of races, has had, and is still having, the most important influence upon the destinies of the human race. It is a principle, laid down by every physiologist, and proved by abundant observation, that man, like other animals, is improved and brought to its highest perfection by an intermingling of the blood and qualities of various races. . . . The great physiological reason why Americans are superior to other nations in freedom, intelligence, and enterprize, is because that they are the offspring of the greatest intermingling of races. . . . The Yankees of New England would never have shown those qualities for which they have been distinguished in war and peace throughout the world had there not been mingled with the puritan English, the calculating Scotch, the warm hearted Irish, the gay and chivalric French, the steady persevering Dutch, and the transcendental Germans, for all these nations contributed to make up the New England character, before the Revolution, and ever since to influence that of the whole American people.

. . . I have yet to learn that foreigners, whether German or Irish, English or French, are at all disposed to do an injury to the asylum which wisdom has prepared and valor won for the oppressed of all nations and religions.

physiology
branch of medicine concerned with the function of the body and its parts

transcendental
concerned with spiritual or philosophical matters

—*Thomas L. Nichols,* Lecture on Immigration and Right of Naturalization, *New York, 1845. Reprinted in William Dudley, series editor,* Opposing Viewpoints in American History, *vol. 1, San Diego: Greenhaven Press, 1996.*

1. Do the examples Nichols gives seem to support universal immigration and the mingling of "races"?

2. In what ways might Nichols's use of *immigration* and *race* seem limited?

"Their Touch Is Pollution": Bayard Taylor's Views on the Chinese

Bayard Taylor was an American poet and journalist who became well known as a travel writer during the mid-nineteenth century. His visits to many parts of the world earned him the nickname "the modern Marco Polo." Taylor's 1855 book about a journey through Asia contained extremely strong opinions about the "national character" of the Chinese people. Like other Americans who shared his anti-Chinese feelings, Taylor feared that the "pure Anglo-Saxon race" could be ruined

Writer Bayard Taylor, shown in this portrait wearing Turkish clothing, traveled through Asia and later warned Americans against "immoral" Chinese immigrants.

by contact with the "pollution" of the Chinese. His hints about the low morals and wicked behavior of the Chinese suggest that he is especially afraid of a sexual mingling of the races—a theme that underlies much anti-immigration propaganda, although it is rarely stated openly.

". . . justice to our own race demands that they should not be allowed to settle on our soil."

IT IS MY DELIBERATE OPINION that the Chinese are, morally, the most debased people on the face of the earth. Forms of vice which in other countries are barely named, are in China so common, that they excite no comment among the natives. They constitute the surface-level, and below them there are deeps on deeps of depravity so shocking and horrible, that their character cannot even be hinted. . . . Their touch is pollution, and, harsh as the opinion may seem, justice to our own race demands that they should not be allowed to settle on our soil.

—*Bayard Taylor,* A Visit to India, China, and Japan, in the Year 1853, *originally published in 1855. Quoted in Stuart Creighton Miller,* The Unwelcome Immigrant: The American Image of the Chinese, 1785–1882, *Berkeley and Los Angeles: University of California Press, 1969.*

THINK ABOUT THIS:

1. Does it seem possible that an entire nation of people could have the worst morals in the world?
2. Do you think that there is such a thing as a national character?

A Senator from Massachusetts Condemns the Chinese Exclusion Act

The Chinese Exclusion Act of 1882 was the first national law that significantly limited immigration. It was also the first to exclude a particular racial, national, or ethnic group. The year the act was passed, nearly 40,000 Chinese arrived in the United States, bringing the country's Chinese population to about 2 million. The following year, after the act had gone into effect, only 8,000 arrived, many of them scholars, diplomats, or businessmen—the act excluded all laborers and farmers. And in 1887 immigration from China totaled fewer than a dozen people. The act expired in 1892, at which time Congress extended it for another ten years. Upon the next expiration, in 1902, Congress extended it indefinitely. The Chinese Exclusion Act was not repealed until 1943. Even in the year it was originally passed, however, not all citizens and lawmakers supported it. Senator George Hoar of Massachusetts spoke out strongly against the Chinese Exclusion Act on the Senate floor. Hoar recognized that the Chinese Exclusion Act was not simply about protecting American jobs—it also grew out of fear based on racial prejudice.

NOTHING IS MORE IN CONFLICT with the genius of American institutions than legal distinctions between individuals based upon race or upon occupation. The framers of our Constitution believed in the safety and wisdom of adherence to abstract principles. They meant that their laws should make no distinction between men except such as were required by personal conduct and character. The prejudice of race, the last of human delusions to be overcome, has been found until lately in our constitutions and statutes, and has left its hideous and ineradicable stains on our history in crimes committed by every generation. . . . But it is reserved for us, at the present day, for the first time, to put into the public law of the world and into the national legislation of the foremost of republican nations a distinction inflicting upon a large class of men a degradation by reason of their race and by reason of their occupation. . . .

"The prejudice of race . . . has left its hideous and ineradicable stains on our history."

The old race prejudice, ever fruitful of crime and of folly, has not been confined to monarchies or to the dark ages. Our own Republic and our own generation have yielded to this delusion, and have paid the terrible penalty.

—From George F. Hoar, Congresssional Record, *47th Congress, 1st Session, 1882, vol. 13. Reprinted in William Dudley, series editor,* Opposing Viewpoints in American History, *vol. 2, San Diego: Greenhaven Press, 1996.*

THINK ABOUT THIS:

1. According to Hoar, the writers of the Constitution wanted the law to make distinctions among people, or treat them differently, only on the basis of "personal conduct and character." What do you think he meant by this?

2. Speaking in 1882, Hoar says that his own country and his own generation have paid a "terrible penalty" because of race prejudice. To what is he referring?

"Let Us Shut the Door": Fears of Race Suicide

Many Americans had no objection to immigration, as long as the great majority of immigrants were white Protestants of British, German, Dutch, or Scandinavian origin. But Roman Catholic immigrants from Ireland disturbed enough Americans to give rise to the Know-Nothing movement in the 1850s, and increased immigration from southern and eastern Europe in the 1880s roused new fears. Critics of immigration warned that Americans were committing "race suicide" by allowing so many foreigners to enter the country. In early 1924, as the U.S. Congress debated whether or not to pass the Johnson-Reed Act, the new law

A notary public works on the sidewalk in a Jewish neighborhood of New York's Lower East Side . . .

. . . while a child peeps from the cellar doorway of a grocery in the Italian neighborhood. The century of immigration made ethnic communities part of the American urban landscape.

that would greatly reduce immigration, Senator Ellison Smith of South Carolina echoed that warning in a speech to his fellow legislators.

I BELIEVE THAT OUR PARTICULAR ideas, social, moral, religious, and political, have demonstrated, by virtue of the progress we have made and the character of people that we are, that we have the highest ideals of any member of the human family or any nation. . . .

I think that we now have a sufficient population in our country for us to shut the door and to breed up a pure, unadulterated American citizenship. I recognize that there is a dangerous lack of distinction between people of a certain nationality and the breed of a dog. . . . Thank God we have in America perhaps the largest percentage of any country in the world of pure unadulterated Anglo Saxon stock. . . . It is for the preservation of that splendid stock that has characterized us that I would make this not an asylum for the oppressed of all countries, but a country to assimilate and perfect that splendid type of manhood that has made the American the foremost nation in her progress and her power, and yet the youngest of all the nations. . . .

Without offense, but with regard to the salvation of our own, let us shut the door. . . .

> ". . . we now have a sufficient population in our country for us to shut the door and to breed up a pure, unadulterated American citizenship."

—*Ellison D. Smith,* Congressional Record, *LXV, part 6. Quoted in Dennis Wepman,*
Immigration: From the Founding of Virginia to the Closing of Ellis Island,
New York: Facts On File, 2002.

THINK ABOUT THIS:

1. What qualities does Smith think make Americans great?
2. Do you think that Smith's opinions display "the highest ideals of any member of the human family"?
3. This speech was made in 1924, not long before Hitler's rise to power in Germany and the beginning of World War II. What statements does it contain that reflect the thinking of the day?

Prejudice: "The Crux of the Immigration Question"

The flood of southern and eastern European immigrants didn't scare all Americans. Some saw them as simply the latest in a long line of new arrivals, facing the same difficulties and criticisms as earlier generations and kinds of immigrants. In an article published in 1914 in a magazine called the *North American Review,* Harvard

Thronged with pushcarts and vendors, Mulberry Street in New York City's Little Italy bustled with immigrant life around 1900.

economics professor A. Piatt Andrew argued that the new immigrants were not hurting the culture, economy, or civic health of the United States.

THE SUBJECT OF IMMIGRATION we have always with us in this country. . . . The Pilgrims and Puritans of Massachusetts Bay were scarcely settled in their log huts before they began planning a policy of exclusion, and already in 1637 they voted to keep out those who were not members of their own religious sect. . . . From that day to this the older immigrants and their descendants have tried to keep this country for those already here and their kindred folk. They have looked upon themselves as a kind of aristocracy, their supposed superiority being proportioned to the length of time that they and their ancestors have lived upon this continent, and each successive generation of immigrants newly arrived has tended with curious repetition to adopt the same viewpoint, to believe that the succeeding immigrants were inferior to the former in religion, habits, education, or what not, and ought to be kept out.

"There is no evidence that the newer immigrants are inferior to the old."

. . . It looks as if in the eyes of some Americans the only good immigrants were the dead immigrants, and that the only opportunities for the country's development lay in the past.

. . . It is easy to echo the cry of prejudice if you happen to be of Anglo-Saxon descent, and to assume an air of superiority and denounce the Italians, Greeks, Poles, Bohemians, and Russian Jews, as if they ranked somewhere between man and the beast, but were not yet wholly human. The same intolerant attitude of mind among the Anglo-Saxon Puritan settlers of early colonial days led to the

Bohemia
central European region that is now part of the Czech Republic

whipping, imprisonment, banishment, and even hanging of Quakers and others of unlike religious beliefs.

. . . There is no evidence that the newer immigrants are inferior to the old. It is only the recurrence of a groundless prejudice which makes some people fear so.

—A. Piatt Andrew, "The Crux of the Immigration Question," North American Review, June 1914. Reprinted in William Dudley, series editor, Opposing Viewpoints in American History, vol. 2, San Diego: Greenhaven Press, 1996.

THINK ABOUT THIS:

1. How does Andrew compare feelings about immigration in his own time with those in the past?
2. According to Andrew, what is the reason for criticism of immigrants?

The *Kroonland* arrives in New York in September 1920, its decks crowded with immigrants eager for their first glimpse of America. Trunks, bundles, and suitcases contain all that they could bring of their former lives. Some immigrants arrived with little more than the clothes they wore—they had sold everything else to pay for their steamship tickets.

Chapter 3

From All the World

THE CENTURY OF IMMIGRATION that ended in 1924 unfolded in several stages. From the beginning of federal immigration records in 1820 through 1860, 5 million people entered the United States—more than 4 million of them between 1840 and 1860. At least 90 percent of all immigrants from 1820 through 1860 were from northwestern Europe. More than half of these were from the British Isles. A million and a half more were German.

Immigration during those decades was more varied than statistics may suggest. People came to the United States from eastern Europe, the Mediterranean lands, and North Africa. The total immigration from these areas, however, was a tiny trickle compared to the flood of northwestern Europeans. The largest group other than the northwestern Europeans came from China. After the discovery of gold in California in 1848, many Chinese scraped together money to emigrate to "Gold Mountain," as they called California, hoping to make their fortunes. Many of them ended up working on crews that built railroads across the mountains and deserts of the West. These Chinese were the first large-scale immigration across the Pacific Ocean. As Ronald Takaki, a scholar of ethnic studies, points out in the title of his 1989 history of Asian Americans, they were *Strangers from a Different Shore.* The discrimination they encountered was caused as much by their skin color and their cultural differences from European Americans as by white Americans' fears of job competition.

Immigration slowed during the early 1860s, when the United States was embroiled in the Civil War, but after the war it quickly returned to its former level—and then surpassed it. The flow of people into the country in the late nineteenth and early twentieth centuries is sometimes called "the new immigration." This new wave of foreigners was more varied than ever. Chinese came until the Chinese Exclusion Act of 1882 closed the door to most of them, but Asian immigration continued with the arrival of people from Japan, Korea, and the Philippines. Immigration from northwestern Europe also continued, but in time it was overshadowed by growing numbers of newcomers from Italy, Spain, Hungary, Greece, Russia, Poland, and other countries in southern and eastern Europe. More than 80 percent of European immigrants in 1907 were southern or eastern Europeans. Arrivals from western Asian countries such as Armenia, Syria, and Turkey also increased, and immigration from other parts of the Americas rose toward significant numbers (in the first quarter of the twentieth century, more than 800,000 Canadians and nearly 300,000 Mexicans moved to the United States). By the time the Immigration Act of 1924 ended America's first century of mass immigra-

A Russian family arrives in New York. Slavs from Poland, Ukraine, Czechoslovakia, Bulgaria, and Russia spoke languages that were different from those of western Europe. Some of these immigrants were Jewish; others followed a distinctively Russian form of Christianity. Despite these differences, Slavic immigrants were able to blend into American society.

tion, the United States had truly received new residents from all the world.

"America as We Imagine It": A Swiss Immigrant's Letter Home

Theodore Bost was born in Switzerland, then lived with his family for a few years in France before emigrating to the United States at the age of seventeen. He lived and worked on farms in rural New York and New Jersey and spent time at a Swiss-run Baptist mission in Canada before taking a job teaching French in Vermont. Just after his twentieth birthday he wrote to his parents, telling them of his ideas for his future.

A NUMBER OF YOUNG MEN from the mission are also thinking of going South, and then, after saving their money for a few years, they plan to go "far in the west" to buy a few hundred acres of land in what, back in Europe, we call America. That is really the only course that is attractive in America. Living in the Eastern states means living a little better than in Europe, but a young man who comes to America as we imagine it back home should go a thousand miles inland.

". . . a young man who comes to America as we imagine it back home should go a thousand miles inland."

. . . In many ways the life of a pioneer, who has to clear the land before he can cultivate it, is terribly hard. His struggle is that of civilization against nature, of civilized people against savages in some places, and of people against wild animals almost everywhere. This struggle is terrifying, especially for people who are no longer young. As for myself, I have no illusions about its difficulties . . . but, after all, when one is young and vigorous and has a strong sense of where one's duty lies, one will be able to overcome the obstacles. Besides, if you expect to harvest a crop, you have to sow it first, and if I hope to have anything to live on in my old age, I shall have to work for it while I'm young.

—*Theodore Bost, 1854, in Ralph H. Bowen, editor and translator,* A Frontier Family in Minnesota: Letters of Theodore and Sophie Bost, *1851–1920, Minneapolis: University of Minnesota Press, 1981.*

THINK ABOUT THIS:

1. What do you think Bost meant by "America as we imagine it back home"?
2. How would you weigh the advantages and disadvantages of going to the frontier, as described by Bost?

Promises to Chinese Emigrants: "All Is Nice"

A large majority of the Asians who immigrated to North America did so through labor recruiters or immigration brokers. These were businessmen whose job it was to sign up workers in countries such as China and deliver them to employers in the United States. Emigrants often had to agree to work for a certain amount of time or had to borrow money from the recruiter to pay for their passage. To attract Chinese emigrants, recruiters spread flyers or posted signs in large coastal cities such as Hong Kong and Shanghai, calling attention to the many benefits of emigrating to America. A Chinese immigration broker circulated this flyer in Hong Kong in 1862.

TO THE COUNTRYMEN OF AU CHEN! There are laborers wanted in the land of Oregon, in the United States of America. There is much inducement to go to this new country, as they have many great works there which are not in our own country. They will supply good houses and plenty of food. They will pay you $28 a month after your arrival, and treat you considerately when you arrive. There is no fear of slavery. All is nice. The ship is now going and will take all who can pay their passage. The money required is $54. Persons having property

Nineteenth-century Chinese immigrants called California "Gold Mountain." Like these laborers panning for gold, many of them sought their fortunes in the mountains and rivers of the American West.

can have it sold for them by correspondents, or borrow money of me upon security; I cannot take security on your children or your wife. Come to me in Hong-Kong and I will care for you until you start.

—*Au Chen, Chinese immigration broker, quoted in Russell H. Conway,* Why the Chinese Emigrate and the Means They Adopt for the Purpose of Reaching America, *New York: Lee & Shepard, 1871. Reprinted in Dennis Wepman,* Immigration: From the Founding of Virginia to the Closing of Ellis Island, *New York: Facts On File, 2002.*

Think about This:

1. If you were thinking about emigrating from China, would you trust Au Chen?

2. Why do you think Au Chen mentions slavery?

From Dalmatia:
John Tadich Crosses the Plains

Among the "new immigrants" who entered the United States in the decades after the Civil War were many Slavs, people who spoke the Slavic languages of Russia and eastern Europe. These included Poles, Czechs, Slovaks, Russians, Bulgarians, Croats, Slovenes, and Serbs. Many of them settled in midwestern cities such as Cleveland and Chicago. Others fanned out across the West. Slavs had come to California in the gold rush of 1849, and for years afterward California continued to draw many Slavic immigrants, who, like most other immigrant groups, generally moved to regions where people from their home communities or regions had already settled. Crossing the Atlantic Ocean was only the first part of their journey. John Tadich, who in 1871 came to California from Dalmatia, an eastern European region that is now part of Croatia, describes the second part.

"We crossed the Mississippi River on a shaky wooden bridge."

FROM NEW YORK WE TRAVELED on the railroad by way of Chicago and Council Bluffs. I remember that there were no dwelling houses in Council Bluffs at that time, just a little shanty for the railroad station. We crossed the Mississippi River on a shaky wooden bridge. Omaha, too, was a small city. . . .The train traveled so slowly that the men of the party were becoming impatient. They were anxious to reach California and start to work; because . . . they were all married men with families left in the old country. . . . I recall now that whenever our train

In 1919, after the end of World War I, Czechoslovakian war brides and their children arrive in the United States. These women had married American soldiers, many of them immigrants from Czechoslovakia who had gone from the United States back to Europe to fight for their native country.

would stop on a side track, hundreds of Indians and their squaws, with papooses on their backs, would gather around the trains. They were just as curious about us as we were about them.

—John V. Tadich, "The Yugoslav Colony of San Francisco on My Arrival in 1871," quoted in Vekoslav Meler, editor, The Diamond Jubilee, 1857–1932, of the Slavonic and Benevolent Mutual Society of San Francisco, San Francisco: The Slavonic Pioneers, 1932.

1. What aspects of the journey across the United States would have been new to an immigrant from eastern Europe?

2. What do you think is the connection between having a family in the old country and being eager to start work?

The Melting-Pot: Israel Zangwill Coins a Powerful Phrase

Israel Zangwill was an English writer whose 1898 novel *The Children of the Ghetto* portrayed Jewish immigrants living in London, England. Ten years later Zangwill turned his attention to the immigrants of America in his best-known work, a play called *The Melting-Pot.* The play is about a tortured romance between two immigrants, a Jewish man and a gentile woman whose people hated each other in Russia, the "old country." They come to see

Jewish immigrants in New York often encountered the same prejudices that they had faced for hundreds of years in Christian Europe. Over time, however, Jews found America a most accepting and welcome home.

Israel Zangwill, shown in his study in England, wrote the play *The Melting-Pot* to share his hopes for a truly multicultural America.

that love conquers hate and that in America immigrants can shed the burden of the past. Zangwill called America a great crucible or melting pot in which God's fire burns away old differences to create a new, united people. The image of the melting pot, of America as a place where people of many kinds blend to form a new society, became one of the most widely used metaphors for immigration. These final lines of the play are spoken as the main characters gaze from a rooftop at the panorama of New York City.

VERA

Look! How beautiful the sunset is after the storm!

DAVID

[Prophetically exalted by the spectacle]

It is the fires of God round His Crucible.

[He drops her hand and looks downward]

There she lies, the great Melting-Pot—listen! Can't you hear the roaring and the bubbling? There gapes her mouth—

[He points east]

—the harbour where a thousand mammoth feeders come from the ends of the world to pour in their human freight. Ah, what a stirring

and a seething! Celt and Latin, Slav and Teuton, Greek and Syrian,—
black and yellow—

VERA

[Softly, nestling to him]

Jew and Gentile—

DAVID

Yes, East and West, and North and South, the palm and the pine, the pole and the equator, the crescent and the cross—how the great Alchemist melts and fuses them with his purging flame! Here shall they all unite to build the Republic of Man and the Kingdom of God! Ah, Vera, what is the glory of Rome and Jerusalem where all nations and races come to worship and look back, compared with the glory of America, where all races and nations come to labour and look forward!

alchemist
someone who practices alchemy, a medieval science and philosophy that aimed, among other things, to transform base metals into gold

—Israel Zangwill, The Melting-Pot: Drama in Four Acts, *New York: Macmillan, 1908.*

THINK ABOUT THIS:

1. In Zangwill's view, what is the desired result of immigration?
2. Why does David think that America is more glorious than Rome and Jerusalem?
3. Do you agree with Zangwill's viewpoint, that an immigrant should look forward, not back?

Jacob Riis Casts an "Unblinking Eye at the Motley Crowd"

Jacob Riis emigrated from Denmark and became a photographer and journalist in the United States. Riis was also a crusader for social reform. His best-known book was *How the Other Half Lives* (1890), which exposed the terrible conditions of America's urban

With photographs such as this one of a Jewish immigrant living in a New York cellar, Danish-American journalist Jacob Riis created powerful primary sources that drew public attention to the misery of the urban poor. Theodore Roosevelt called Riis "the best American I ever knew."

slums, especially in New York City. Riis returned to the topic several decades later in *The Battle with the Slum*. In a chapter titled "On Whom Shall We Shut the Door?" he considers the flow of "new emigrants" through the receiving station that was established in 1892 on Ellis Island in New York Harbor.

THE JEW AND THE ITALIAN HAVE FILLED the landscape so far, because, as a matter of fact, that is what they do. Yesterday it was the Irishman and the Bohemian. To-morrow it may be the Greek, who already undersells the Italian from his pushcart in the Fourth Ward, and the Syrian, who can give Greek, Italian, and Jew points at a trade. The rebellious Slovak holds his own corner in our industrial system. . . . From Dalmatia comes a new emigration, and there are signs that the whole Balkan peninsula has caught the fever and is waiting only for cheap transportation to be established on the Danube [River] to the Black Sea, when there is no telling what may be heading our way. I sometimes wonder what thoughts come to the eagle that perches over the great stone gateway on Ellis Island, as he watches the procession that files through it in the United States, day after day, and never ends. He looks out of his grave, unblinking eye at the motley crowd, but gives no sign.

A Syrian grocery shop in New York, 1919. The increased number of immigrants from the Middle East was creating new ethnic communities in American cities.

. . . Fear not, eagle! While that gate is open let no one bar the one you guard. While the flag flies . . . keep it aloft over Ellis Island and have no misgivings.

—*Jacob Riis,* The Battle with the Slum, *New York: Macmillan & Co., 1912.*

THINK ABOUT THIS:

1. Does this selection suggest that Riis is for immigration or against it?
2. How might Riis's background as an immigrant and social reformer have influenced his description of the various kinds of immigrants?

Chapter 4

Leaving Home

IN 1922 MARGE GLASGOW EMIGRATED from her home in Motherwell, Scotland. "My whole idea," she told an interviewer years later, "was to get to [the] United States, and work, and help bring my family. . . . I had no relatives in America. . . . It wasn't easy for me to convince my parents that I was capable of going over and taking care of myself. But I was determined. . . . I finally got my way." Glasgow was fifteen years old when she made the ten-day ocean crossing. Once she had arrived in America, she recalled, "I began to have regrets about leaving home. I was feeling very lonesome, sorry for myself, crying all the time." Glasgow soon adjusted to her new surroundings, but her brush with homesickness and unhappiness was something that many immigrants experienced. Coming to America wasn't just the beginning of a new life—it also meant saying good-bye to the old life.

Sometimes families emigrated together. They had to say farewell to homes, friends, relatives, familiar surroundings, and beloved possessions, but at least they still had each other. Often,

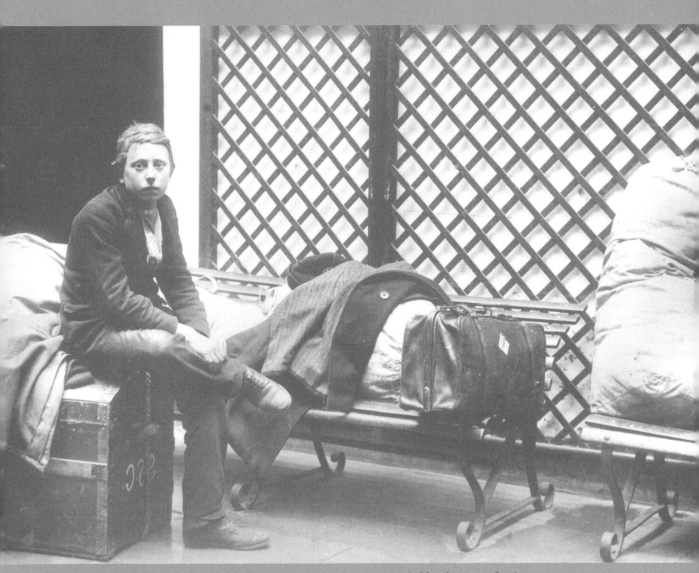

Being alone could make an immigrant's journey difficult, even frightening.
Still, many men and boys—and women and girls, too—crossed the ocean
by themselves. Some came to America so that they could earn money to send home
to their families, hoping to be reunited with their loved ones someday. Others,
like this Italian youth, were orphans who planned to build
new lives in new surroundings.

however, one family member, like Marge Glasgow, emigrated first, hoping to earn money to send home so that the rest could follow. Some families were separated for years before being reunited. And some separations were permanent. In 1871 a German immigrant named Heinrich Möller wrote to his mother and father, "Dear parents! If God grants me life we will meet again before 2 years have passed, for then I will come to Germany to get you, then you will be near me." Busy with a house, farm, and growing family, Möller never made that journey. Nine years later he wrote:

> Dearly beloved parents, I have received your letter and learned from it that your end is near, or perhaps by the time this letter reaches you, it will already be too late, I hope not since my greatest desire is to see you again, dear father, I have had no peace of mind for years now, I always think about coming back to Germany again but times have been so bad. . . . I haven't given up all hope of seeing you again. If it is not God's will, we'll have to accept it and hope to meet if not in this world than in the next.

For many emigrants, even those most eager to reach the United States, the act of leaving home brought both sadness and joy. Even after they became established in their new homes in America, some longed to see again the places and people they had left behind. At the same time, people in the old countries eagerly awaited letters and visits from the emigrants. By telling of their successes in America, the land of golden opportunity, some of those who had already left home inspired others to follow in their footsteps.

A Chinese Boy Hears of the "American Wizards"

Not everyone who left his or her homeland intended to stay away forever. Many emigrants simply wanted to work in America for a time, save their money, and return to their former homes able to live better than they had before. Some achieved this dream. Lee Chew, an immigrant from China, described the return of a successful emigrant to his native village in China.

[WHEN] I WAS ABOUT sixteen years of age, a man of our tribe came back from America and took ground as large as four city blocks and made a paradise of it. He put a large stone wall around and led some streams through it and built a palace and summer house and about twenty other structures. . . . The man had gone away from our village a poor boy. Now he returned with unlimited wealth, which he had obtained in the country of the American wizards. . . . Having made his wealth among the barbarians this man had faithfully returned to pour it out among his tribesmen, and he is living in our village now very happy, and a pillar of strength to the poor.

"Having made his wealth among the barbarians this man had faithfully returned to pour it out among his tribesmen."

—Lee Chew, "Life Story of a Chinaman," in Hamilton Holt, editor, *The Life Stories of Undistinguished Americans as Told by Themselves, New York: James Pott & Co., 1906.*

1. Why do you think the Chinese villagers called Americans "wizards" and "barbarians"?
2. What effect might this emigrant's return have had on Lee Chew and other villagers?

"Oleana": A Dream Becomes a Disaster

Many emigrants planned to settle near people from their communities or regions who had already established themselves in the United States. Ethnic settlements or neighborhoods naturally grew up in many parts of the United States. In a few cases, however,

migrations were organized with the goal of founding ethnic colonies in America. One such plan was that of Ole Bull, a world-famous violinist from Norway. Bull wanted to sponsor the emigration of poor rural Norwegians to America, and in 1852 he bought a large tract of land in Pennsylvania and announced that the colony

Famous Norwegian musician Ole Bull tried and failed to establish an ideal immigrant colony.

of Oleana was open for settlement. Oleana failed within a year, partly because Bull had not ensured legal ownership of the land and partly because the land itself was hilly, rocky, and generally unsuitable for farming. In 1853 a Norwegian comic writer named Ditmar Meidell immortalized the episode in the song "Oleana," poking fun at outlandish claims about the easy life in America. The song was immensely popular both in Norway and among Norwegians in Pennsylvania, many of whom moved on to settle in Wisconsin and Minnesota.

I'm off to Oleana, I'm turning from my doorway,
No chains for me, I'll say good-bye to slavery in Norway.
They give you land for nothing in jolly Oleana,
And grain comes leaping from the ground in floods of
golden manna.

. . . .

The crops they are gigantic, potatoes are immense, Sir,
You make a quart of whiskey from each one without
expense, Sir.

. . . .

And cakes come raining down, Sir, with chocolate frosting
coated,
They're nice and rich and sweet, good Lord, you eat them
till you're bloated.

. . . .

Support your wife and kids? Why, the count [nobleman or
governor] pays for that, Sir,

You'd slap officials down and out if they should leave you
    flat, Sir.

. . . . . .

And so we play the fiddle, and all of us are glad, Sir,
We dance a merry polka, boys, and that is not so bad, Sir.
I'm off to Oleana, to lead a life of pleasure,
A beggar here, a count out there, with riches in full
    measure.
Ole—Ole—Ole—oh! Oleana!
Ole—Ole—Ole—oh! Oleana!

—Translated and quoted in Leola Nelson Bergmann, Americans from Norway,
New York and Philadelphia: J. B. Lippincott Co., 1950.

THINK ABOUT THIS:

1. How would you describe the tone of "Oleana"?
2. What ideas about America are reflected in the song?

Talking and Going Are Two Different Things: Notes from a Welshman

Many emigrants felt a strong desire to tell the folks back home
about their experiences. They wrote letters—or, if they could not
read and write, found others to write for them. Most letters were to
family members, such as this letter from a Welsh emigrant named
John Lloyd to his parents in his home village. Sometimes, in order
to share their experiences with the largest possible number of interested readers back home, emigrants wrote to the newspapers of

Emigrants' letters were read and reread by those left behind, as shown in Irish artist James Brennan's 1875 painting *Letter from America*.

their former towns and cities, which published their letters. Printed in papers or passed from hand to hand, emigrants' letters were a valuable source of information for others who were thinking about making the journey. They communicated useful, practical details—and sometimes they prepared their readers for the emotional strains and surprises that awaited the emigrant.

August 1, 1868

Ha! Ha! here I am at last with my feet on the famous land of America. Many laughed at me when I said I was coming here and said, "We will believe you when you have gone." Well, will they believe me now because I have gone.

. . . Talking about going to America and actually going are two different things. Many of my friends came to see me off down the river. They looked worriedly at me and I at them. It was a shaky first step from the landing stage onto the ship. As we sailed those who were left behind waved their handkerchiefs, their hands and

"Many laughed at me when I said I was coming here and said, 'We will believe you when you have gone.'"

their hats above their heads. . . . Soon we could see the shores of Flintshire, and when opposite Rhyl, ah! there was the dear Clwyd Valley as if opening before me and a feeling of *hiraeth* [roughly, "nostalgia"] came over me as I remembered the Pont'ralltgoch lay in that direction and as I caught sight of the haunts of my youth I shed a tear.

—*Quoted in Alan Conway, editor,* The Welsh in America: Letters from the Immigrants, *Minneapolis: University of Minnesota Press, 1961.*

Think about This:

What emotions does Lloyd reveal in this part of his letter? How do you think he feels about his decision to emigrate?

Immigrants Helping Emigrants: "I Wish I Could Go with You"

Once they had established themselves in the United States, immigrants often sent advice and money to help family members and friends follow them. Some returned to their former homes to bring others back to America with them. The story of young John Tadich, who was brought as a boy to California from his home in Dalmatia, shows how networks of relatives and friends aided emigrants.

ON THE TWENTY SECOND DAY OF MAY, in the year 1871, I left my native town of Starigrad, in Dalmatia, on the beautiful eastern coast of the Adriatic Sea. . . . Bidding farewell to my mother, I started on my long journey, my father and brother accompanying me as far as Split. We had to go first to . . . meet Lorenzo Nizetich, a pioneer miner of Sutter Creek, Amador County, California, who was returning to California, and whose party my uncle, Nicholas Buja (already in California) had advised me to join. We arrived at the Nizetich home about noontime and found a good lunch prepared for us. I remember well that after the lunch I went outside like any young boy would do, to play with a group of children in front of the church. The other boys were strangers to me; but they all knew that I was the boy who was going to California with Lorenzo Nizetich. One of the boys came very close to me and asked many questions about my trip to California and I recall that he said to me with sadness in his voice: "Oh, I wish I could go with you."

—*John V. Tadich, "The Yugoslav Colony of San Francisco on My Arrival in 1871," quoted in Vekoslav Meler, editor,* The Diamond Jubilee, 1857–1932, *of the Slavonic and Benevolent Mutual Society of San Francisco, San Francisco: The Slavonic Pioneers, 1932.*

THINK ABOUT THIS:

Why might the parents of a young boy have allowed him to go to California?

An Irish Family on the Move

When eighteen-year-old Catherine Moran emigrated from Ireland to Boston in 1903, her journey was just one of many departures—and partings—her family had made over the years. As her story shows, America was not the only destination for emigrants. Many people who left England, Scotland, or Ireland went to other British territories, such as Australia or Canada. Some Europeans and some Asians also emigrated to South American nations such as Peru, Argentina, and Uruguay. But the United States, during its century of immigration, was the chief destination of people who, like the Morans, wanted to change their lives.

THERE WAS TWELVE IN OUR FAMILY. The oldest died and the other one went to Australia with my uncle. I was about five when she went. So there was ten of us, you might say, in our family. We had to pay *every cent* we could possibly produce to pay taxes. . . .

We wasn't put out of our land because I had brothers. Some of them were old enough to work and just pay back the rent. Just *exist,* try to exist.

My mother kept house and my father had no work but just the bit of land we had, to work it,

Economic hardship in Ireland led many families to emigrate—not just to the United States but also to Canada and Australia.

and give the cream of the milk to England for everything. They had to get the big rent, and then if the year was bad and the stuff didn't grow, we suffered. . . .

When I went to school, we couldn't have any shoes; we had to save and give it to the rent. . . .

"The one who came here first was a brother. . . . Then there was my sister."

It was only about ten dollars or some-thin' to come [to the United States] at that time. It was cheap. I'm here seventy-three years. My sister's here seventy-five. Once she's here she sent for me, see. There was five of us out here.

The one who came here first was a brother, and he would be out here six years, and he went back home. Then there was my sister. . . .

I came by myself, except you might meet someone on the boat was from nearby, but you wouldn't know them at home. I was eight-een in April, and I come, I think, May or June.

—*Catherine Moran McNamara, interview, in June Namias,* First Generation: In the Words of Twentieth-Century American Immigrants, *Boston: Beacon Press, 1978.*

THINK ABOUT THIS:

1. Does this passage suggest why so many members of the Moran family left their homeland?
2. What might Moran have liked about living in the United States?

From Korea to Hawaii in 1905

Paik Kuang Sun was born in Korea in 1900. Five years later, after Japan began a military occupation of Korea that lasted for many years, the Paik family was forced from its house. Soon afterward, the Paiks left their country. Paik Kuang Sun—later known as Mary Paik—was only five years old at the time, but later she wrote an account of her family's emigration and her life in Hawaii and California. As her story shows, some of those who came to America were driven out of their homelands by forces beyond their control.

ONE AFTERNOON IN 1905, as I was waiting on the front steps for Grandfather, I saw two men attired in strange-looking clothes walking towards our house. As they stopped at our gate, I ran into the house to call Grandmother. She came out to meet them. After a few minutes she returned, looking very serious, and said that we had to move out right away. This caused much talk and excitement during the evening meal. It turned out that the two strange men were Japanese officers, and they wanted everyone to move out so that they could use our home to house their soldiers. As Grandmother told about the Japanese soldiers, our family sat in stunned silence. Although the news was no surprise to them, it must have felt as though the sky had fallen on us. Soon friends came over, asking what should be done. The only choice was to leave that night or stay and live with the soldiers in our home, which no one wanted to do. I don't remember any of the details of what happened that night. It was so confusing.

. . . The family decided to go to Inchon, the nearest large city with a harbor, to see what we could do for a living there. It took several days and nights of walking with very little rest to reach our destination. We could only bring our bedding, clothes, and food for the journey. Father must have carried me on his back, but I must have slept most of the way because I don't remember anything about the trip. . . .

There happened to be two ships in Inchon harbor, sent by owners of sugar cane plantations in Hawaii to recruit workers. People were told that if a man signed a contract to work for one year, he and his family would be given free passage to Hawaii. After that, he would be free to go wherever he wished. His wages were to be fifty cents per day, working from dawn to dusk. Father signed on, and that was how we went to Hawaii on the S.S. *Siberia,* arriving on May 8, 1905.

"His wages were to be fifty cents per day, working from dawn to dusk."

—*Mary Paik Lee,* Quiet Odyssey: A Pioneer Korean Woman in America, *edited by Sucheng Chan, Seattle: University of Washington, 1990.*

THINK ABOUT THIS:

1. Why do you think the narrator's father signed the labor contract?

2. Can you think of other examples of people driven out of their homes by invasion or occupation?

Most emigrants traveled in steerage, the least expensive, most crowded
quarters on the ships. Conditions were often terrible belowdecks, so when
weather permitted, the passengers spent time in the open air.

Chapter 5

Passages and Arrivals

EXCEPT FOR THOSE WHO CAME BY LAND from Canada and Mexico, all arrivals to the United States during the century of immigration came by passenger ship. Some could afford to travel more or less comfortably. Many emigrants, however, could barely scrape together the money to pay for the cheapest passage available. They traveled in what is known as steerage—which meant that their quarters were more crowded and less sanitary, and their food less wholesome and less appetizing, than those of first- or second-class passengers. Despite laws meant to improve the treatment of steerage passengers, many emigrants endured miserable conditions on their way to the new country. In 1853, a group of Norwegians who had emigrated to the United States were so outraged that they wrote to a Norwegian newspaper, warning their fellow countrymen and countrywomen, "All of us have suffered so much hardship and seen so much evil during our passage from Liverpool to America on the English [ships] this year that we feel it is our duty, without delay, to inform you of this."

Occasionally, shipboard conditions became nightmarish. Vessels could be crowded and filthy. Outbreaks of disease among the steerage passengers could bring suffering and death. Even on easier voyages, emigrants confronted the ordinary difficulties of ocean travel, such as seasickness and storms. Yet some travelers enjoyed their first sea voyages and their first glimpses of a world larger than their village or neighborhood.

Throughout the century of immigration, the majority of immigrants arrived in New York City, the biggest harbor in the United States. To make their entry more orderly and to provide basic services such as money changing to the new arrivals, the city opened a

Ships and boats line the docks of Manhattan (*right*) and New Jersey (*left*) in this 1880s view of the Hudson River and New York's bustling piers.

receiving station called Castle Garden in 1855. States and cities opened similar sta-

Opened in 1855, Castle Garden was New York's receiving station for immigrants until the 1890s.

tions in other ports, such as Boston and New Orleans, but Castle Garden remained the busiest. With the number of immigrants continuing to rise, the federal government took control of immigration from the states in 1890, establishing the Bureau of Immigration to oversee the newcomers' entry into the country. The bureau closed Castle Garden, which had become run-down, and built a new federal receiving station on Ellis Island in New York Harbor. It opened in 1892. For the rest of the century of immigration, Ellis Island was the main point of entry. The government closed it in 1954 because immigration had decreased and many of those who did come now arrived by air. Today a museum of immigration stands on the island where once thousands of immigrants nervously awaited the inspections and formalities that would let them enter the country. A third important receiving station, Angel Island in San Francisco Bay, was opened in 1910 to control immigration from Asia and remained in use until 1940.

A Voice from the Steerage

Liverpool was one of England's major shipping ports. During the century of immigration, its ships carried hundreds of thousands of immigrants from England and all over Europe to the United States. One who made that journey was William Smith, who crossed the Atlantic in 1847–1848 and soon afterward wrote a book about his experiences. His "disastrous voyage" included, among other problems, disease aboard the ship, a serious water shortage, and bad food.

ship-fever
one of several infectious diseases that broke out on ships, including typhoid and cholera

hogshead
large barrel

MOST OF THOSE WHO HAD DIED of ship-fever were delirious, some a day, others only a few hours previous to death. . . .

When we had been at sea a month, the steward discovered the four hogsheads, by oversight or neglect, had not been filled. On the following morning . . . our water was reduced from two quarts to one quart per day for an adult and one pint for a child. . . . I had nothing but ship allowances to subsist upon, which was scarcely sufficient to keep us from perishing, being only a pound of sea-biscuit (full of maggots) and a pint of water. . . . I was seized with ship-fever, at first I was so dizzy that I could not walk without danger of falling; . . . my brains felt as if they were on fire, . . . and my lips were parched with excessive thirst.

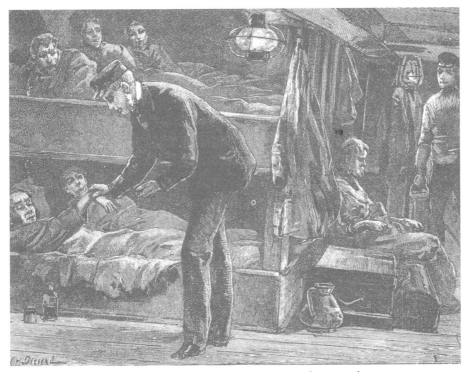

A ship's doctor examines a sick emigrant. Crowding and poor sanitation turned some emigrants' passages into nightmares of disease.

This disastrous voyage [came] to an end, after an absence of exactly eight weeks from the shores of my native land. . . . My whole lifetime did not seem so long as the last two months appeared to me.

—*William Smith,* An Immigrant's Narrative; or a Voice from the Steerage, *New York: W. Smith, 1850.*

THINK ABOUT THIS:

Would you be willing to undergo an ordeal such as Smith's to come to America?

"The Ship Was Our World": Mary Antin Crosses the Atlantic

In 1894 thirteen-year-old Mary Antin, her mother, and her siblings left their home in Poland to join Antin's father, who had emigrated to the United States three years earlier. Antin saw the journey as "a tremendous adventure." Later she published autobiographical articles about her experiences in the magazine *Atlantic Monthly,* and in 1912 the articles were collected into a book called *The Promised Land.* It described every step of Antin's journey, starting with the awe and envy of playmates in her Jewish neighborhood in Poland when they learned that she was going to America, continuing with the family's reunion in Boston, and including her thoughts, years later, about how being an immigrant had shaped her life. Antin wrote, "All the processes of uprooting, transportation, replanting, acclimatization, and development took place in my own soul." Here she describes boarding the ship and making the ocean voyage, which she had also described in a letter to her uncle.

OUR TURN CAME AT LAST. We were conducted through the gate of departure, and after some hours of bewildering manoeuvres . . . we found ourselves—we five frightened pilgrims from Polotzk—on the deck of a great big steamship afloat on the strange big waters of the ocean.

For sixteen days the ship was our world. My letter dwells solemnly on the details of life at sea, as if afraid to cheat my uncle of the smallest circumstance. It does not shrink from describing the torments of seasickness; it notes every change in the weather. A rough night is described, when the ship pitched and rolled so that people were thrown from their berths; days and nights when we crawled through dense fogs, our foghorns drawing answering warnings from invisible ships. The perils of the sea were not minimized in the imaginations of us inexperienced voyagers. The captain and his officers ate their dinners, smoked their pipes and slept soundly in their turns, while we frightened emigrants turned our faces to the wall and awaited our watery graves.

". . . we frightened emigrants turned our faces to the wall and awaited our watery graves."

All this while the seasickness lasted. Then came happy hours on deck, with fugitive sunshine, birds atop the crested waves, band music and dancing and fun. I explored the ship, made friends with officers and crew, or pursued my thoughts in quiet nooks. It was my first experience of the ocean, and I was profoundly moved.

—*Mary Antin,* The Promised Land, *Boston and New York: Houghton Mifflin Company, 1912.*

THINK ABOUT THIS:

1. Were Mary Antin's moods during the voyage influenced by outside forces? If so, what were those forces?

2. How do you think Mary's age might have affected how she felt about the voyage?

"Unfortunate Travellers": A Chinese Immigrant's Poem of Consolation

After 1882, the Chinese Exclusion Act limited immigration from China to students and teachers, businesspeople, diplomats and other government officials, temporary visitors, and American citizens—including relatives of Chinese people who had been born in the United States. Many of those who came to the country posed as students, teachers, or sons of American-born Chinese. Desperate to reach America, they used phony documents and memo-

Asian immigrants arrived at San Francisco's Angel Island, called the "Ellis Island of the West."

Waiting to enter the United States, immigrants carved poems of frustration into the wooden walls of Angel Island's detention center.

rized the details of their "families." This was necessary because they faced strict examinations at Angel Island. If they failed to convince the immigration officials that they qualified to be admitted, they would be held on the island and then returned to China. The examination process itself could drag on for months. Some of those who waited, bored or frustrated or outraged, wrote poems in Chinese on the walls of their dormitories in the barracks of Angel Island station, a former military base.

Over one hundred poems are on the walls.
Looking at them, they are all pining at the delayed
    progress.
What can one sad person say to another?
Unfortunate travellers everywhere wish to **commiserate**.
Gain or lose, how is one to know what is **predestined**?
Rich or poor, who is to say it is not the will of heaven?
Why should one complain if he is detained and
    imprisoned here?
From ancient times, heroes were often the first ones to
    face adversity.

commiserate
show sympathy

predestined
fated to be

—*"Poem by One Named Xu, From Xiangshan, Consoling Himself,"* quoted in Hiam Mark Lai, Genny Lim, and Judy Yung, Island: Poetry and History of Chinese Immigrants on Angel Island, 1910–1940, *Chinese Culture Foundation of San Francisco, 1980.*

THINK ABOUT THIS:

1. How would you describe the speaker's mood?
2. Does the speaker find anything positive in his situation? If so, what?

Evelyn Berkowitz: A Passage from Hungary

Evelyn Berkowitz's family emigrated from a small town in Hungary in 1921. She was twelve—old enough to be aware of conditions on the *Mongolia,* the ship that carried her family and many other immigrants.

FIRST OF ALL, EVERYBODY GOT SICK. It was rough seas. For five days I was laid up. I didn't eat a thing. I was the worst. The little ones would throw up, and then they were all right. My brother came in eating a piece of bread from the lunchroom and he said, "Oh, this piece of bread tastes awful." Next thing, he starts throwing up.

There were also rats on the boat. I was on the upper bunk, and there were pipes above. And the rats were just running back and forth on those pipes. One day, Dad hit one on the tail, and that thing was squeaking so far. After that we got relief, because usually when they get hurt they don't come back to that same spot. It wasn't a nice boat.

"It wasn't a nice boat."

Then a couple of days out, the ship sprung a hole and water was coming in. In fact, we were walking around with our life jackets. They sent an SOS out, and told us another ship was coming to help us. But before that ship got to us, they fixed the hole, and we kept on going. In New York they reported in the paper that the *Mongolia* sunk, and all the people went down. When we got to New York, they couldn't believe it. They said we were found people, that the boat went down.

We arrived in New York late December 1921. We were eleven days on ship. When we saw that Statue of Liberty, everybody started screaming and crying and hollering, they were just so happy to see it, to be in America. By this time I was feeling better and it was such a thrill to see it. Then for one week we waited in New York Harbor, because a lot of other ships had come in and we had to wait our turn.

—*Evelyn Berkowitz, interview, in Peter Morton Coan,* Ellis Island Interviews: In Their Own Words, *New York: Facts On File, 1997.*

Think about This:

1. Evelyn says that people in New York called the *Mongolia*'s passengers "found people." What do you think this means?

2. What might Evelyn's feelings have been during the week the ship waited in the harbor?

A Greek Immigrant Remembers Ellis Island

Theodore Spako was sixteen years old in 1911, when he left his home and parents to go to the United States. Years later he told an

More than 12 million immigrants arrived at Ellis Island between 1892 and 1954.

interviewer about the journey, during which he befriended Gus, a fellow Greek, and Gus's father. Like all arrivals, they faced examination on Ellis Island. Some who hoped to enter were turned away because they did not pass medical tests or some other requirement. The examinations were a great source of anxiety and, for those who were refused entry, despair.

WE LANDED IN NEW YORK after twenty-two days at sea. I remember we see Statue of Liberty. Gus ask me, "What's the statue?" And then we're looking at the statue, and his father say, "That's Christopher Columbus." And I put my two cents out. I say, "Listen, this don't look like Christopher Columbus. That's a lady out there."

"I just thank God. To this day I pray, dear Lord, and thank God, that I was admitted to the United States."

Everybody was hungry, and they started examinations on Ellis Island. I had twenty-five dollars in my pocket. I knew to bring money, otherwise they keep you there. They wouldn't let you go to shore without money. Because if you were hungry, you might steal. And I was alongside Gus, and noticed he had a chalk mark on his back. I couldn't reach or see my own back, so I asked him, "Do I have a chalk mark on the back?" So he looked, he says, "No." I say, "You've got one. Your father, too." And I'm thinking, either they go back to Greece or I go back to Greece. So what happened, the one with the chalk mark went back to Greece. Gus and his father went back. I don't know why.

I just thank God. To this day I pray, dear Lord, and thank God,

The Eye Examination Room at Ellis Island, 1912. Some of the men's jackets are chalk-marked with Xs. This means that examiners consider these arrivals to have a "suspected mental defect" that could prevent them from entering the country.

that I was admitted to the United States, that they didn't put a chalk mark on my back.

—*Theodore Spako, interview, quoted in Peter Morton Coan,* Ellis Island Interviews: In Their Own Words, *New York: Facts On File, 1997.*

THINK ABOUT THIS:

What could officials at Ellis Island have done differently to reduce the anxiety that Spako and other immigrants felt?

Chapter 6

Life in the New Country

ONCE THEY HAD ENTERED the United States, immigrants had to deal with the same concerns of everyday life as citizens. They sought out homes, food, clothing, and jobs. They navigated unfamiliar neighborhoods and learned how to get around, shop, and communicate. They dealt with family life, school, and romance. Many of them did all this with no knowledge of English, the chief language of their adopted home. All of them had to make a thousand adjustments, large and small, to new circumstances, laws, and freedoms. And some of them had to cope with the added obstacle of ethnic or racial prejudice. Some immigrants found the experience of plunging into a new and unfamiliar world to be an exhilarating adventure. For others, it was stressful, even frightening at times.

Several things helped cushion immigrants from the shock of being transplanted. Many immigrants were linked together in networks of friends and relatives, with those who came first offering advice and help to those who came later. Immigrants found comfort in the ethnic neighborhoods and communities that

Many immigrant women earned money by doing piecework, such as sewing, ironing, or making decorative buttons, for which they were paid by the piece. These children are helping their mother work in their tenement home in New York City, 1905.

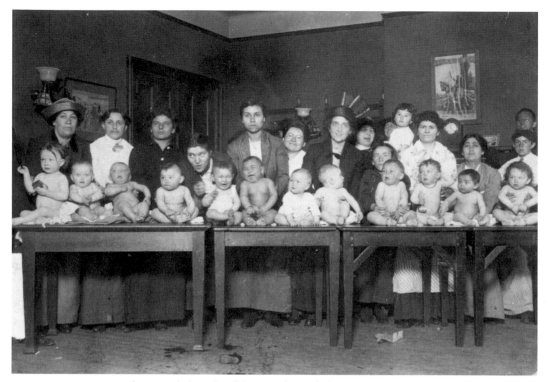

Immigrant mothers and their healthy newborn babies at New York's University Settlement, a center of social services for immigrants and the poor that opened in 1886. It was part of the settlement house movement, which originated in England in the early 1880s and inspired middle-class volunteers to live with, assist, and educate the urban poor.

formed as people from the same points of origin settled near one another in the United States. Whether in San Francisco's Chinatown, New York's Little Italy, or the Scandinavian towns of Minnesota, newcomers could speak in their native languages, buy familiar foods, and share their traditional holidays and customs with others from the same backgrounds. Immigrants helped one another in more practical ways, too. Many ethnic groups formed self-help societies that collected dues and used the money to make loans or charitable gifts to members and to pay their funeral expenses. Loans raised in this way helped many immigrants start their own businesses, go to college, or buy land.

Challenging though life in America could be, most immigrants accepted the challenges gladly. They had given up much and endured much to reach the United States, with all its perils and promises. They realized that their journey of change and discovery would continue long after they had stepped ashore.

Enjoying Equality: A Former Englishman Writes Home

Some immigrants to the United States were greatly pleased to find themselves living under political and social systems very different from those of their native countries. Early in the century of immigration Joseph Hollingsworth wrote to an aunt and uncle in Yorkshire, England, expressing his satisfaction with life in America.

South Leicester, Dec. 7th, 1828

Respected Aunt & Uncle,
This day being the 1st Anniversary of my landing in America I wanted to celebrate it by writing a Letter.

I have lived in America exactly one year. I have seen all the Seasons and must confess that I prefer the American weather far before the English. I have never seen in this Country a Beggar such as I used Daily to see in England, nor a tax gatherer with his *Red Book* as Impudent as the D-v-l, taking the last penny out of the poor Mans Pocket. In this country are no Lords, nor Dukes, nor

Counts, nor Marquises, nor Earls, no Royal Family to support nor no King. The "President of the United States" is the highest Titled fellow in this Country. He is chosen by the people, out of the People; holds his station four years, and if not rechosen he is no more than the rest of the People. The President when he makes a speech does not begin with "My Lords and Gentlemen" but with "Fellow Citizens."

"In this country are no Lords, nor Dukes, . . . no Royal Family to support nor no King."

. . . The more I live in this Country the better I like it. . . . You must excuse my Brothers James and Jabez for not writing as they are both deeply engaged in Sparking.

sparking
courting,
wooing

. . . We are all in good Health at present hoping you are the same. Jabez & James are a little tickled at what I have Just written So I will conclude.

I Remain your most Inteligent
Affectionate & well Wishing Nephew

—Quoted in Noel Rae, editor, Witnessing America: The Library of Congress Book of Firsthand Accounts of Life in America 1600–1900. Harmondsworth, England: Penguin, 1996.

THINK ABOUT THIS:

Judging from these paragraphs, what do you think Hollingsworth misses least about England?

Mother Jones: An Immigrant Woman and the Labor Movement

Mary Harris was a child when she came to the United States from Ireland. When she grew up she taught school and ran a dressmaking business in Chicago, then married George Jones, an ironworker, and settled with him in Memphis, Tennessee. After her husband died in an 1867 epidemic, she became involved in the struggle of American laborers to form unions and win the right to strike for better wages and working conditions. Until her death at the age of a hundred, Mother Jones, as she became known, was vigorously active in the labor movement, arranging strikes, demonstrations, marches, and meetings in support of workers and their unions.

I WAS BORN IN THE CITY of Cork, Ireland, in 1830. My people were poor. For generations they had fought for Ireland's freedom. Many of my folks have died in that struggle. My father, Richard Harris, came to America in 1835, and as soon as he had become an American citizen he sent for his family. . . . Here I was brought up, but always as the child of an American citizen. Of that citizenship I have ever been proud.

. . . In 1867, a yellow fever epidemic swept Memphis. Its victims were mainly

"I'm not a humanitarian," Mother Jones once told an audience. "I'm a hell-raiser." For decades Mary Harris Jones, an Irish immigrant, helped lead the labor movement in America. She fought for better conditions and pay for coal-mine workers, who called her "The Miner's Angel."

among the poor and the workers. The rich and the well-to-do fled the city.

. . . After the union had buried my husband, I got a permit to nurse the sufferers. This I did until the plague was stamped out.

I returned to Chicago and went again into the dressmaking business. . . . We worked for the aristocrats of Chicago, and I had ample opportunity to observe the luxury and extravagance of their lives. Often while sewing for the lords and barons who lived in magnificent houses on the Lake Shore Drive, I would look out of the plate glass windows and see the poor, shivering wretches, jobless and hungry, walking along the frozen lake front. The contrast of their condition with that of the tropical comfort of the people for whom I sewed was painful to me. My employers seemed neither to notice nor to care.

—*Mary Field Parton, editor,* The Autobiography of Mother Jones, *Chicago: Charles H. Keer & Co., 1925.*

THINK ABOUT THIS:

1. Do you think that Mother Jones's description of her Irish heritage is significant? How might her background have influenced her?
2. Based on the actions she mentions in this excerpt, what kind of a person do you think Jones was?

Missing the Homeland: The Irish "Song of the Exile"

Even immigrants who had eagerly embraced the opportunity to start new lives in America often expressed sadness at the thought of what they had left behind. Irish immigrants sang sorrowful songs such as "Song of the Exile," written by James Gibbons in 1843 for

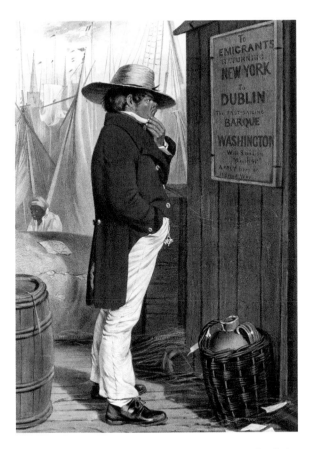

Titled *Homeward Bound, The Quay of New York*, this 1854 illustration depicts the dream of the homesick Irish immigrant who thinks about sailing from New York back to Dublin.

a celebration on Saint Patrick's Day, an important Irish holiday. The lyric touches on themes found in many Irish immigrant songs. One is a longing for the beauties of Ireland, here called Erin. Another is the grief of the immigrant, or exile, who remains emotionally tied to the homeland even when far away. A third is concern over political events in Ireland, which was struggling to win independence from Great Britain.

Hail, thrice happy day to the exile endearing
As he wanders afar o'er life's troubled sea,
And sacred's the tie that still binds him to Erin,
While the pulse of his heart throbs for Cushlamachree.
No hills are so green as my own native mountains,
No valley so fertile, no flowers so fair;

No nectar more pure than thy crystal-like fountains,
Whose murmurs are fanned by thine own balmy air.

Behold our loved Erin in bold agitation,
Combating with despots to sever her chains,
Proclaiming aloud that she must be a nation,
Free as the breezes that sweep over her plains.
Nations have sunk 'neath the lash of oppression,
Their glory departed all shrouded in gloom,
Whilst Erin Mavourneen resisting aggression
Thy spirit ne'er slumbered in slavery's
    tomb.

Oh! Harp of my country, the pride of her
    sages,
In vain would the tyrant thy numbers
    control.
Thou'rt the gift of our fathers, the boast of
    past ages,
Thy music still lives in each Irishman's soul.
Then hail to thee, Erin! wherever I wander,
My spirit still lingers round thy loved shore,
Where nature appears in her own native grandeur,
And thy sons are as brave as their fathers of yore.

"Oh! Harp of my country. . . . Thy music still lives in each Irishman's soul."

—*Reprinted in Robert R. Grimes, S.J.,* How Shall We Sing in a Foreign Land?
Music of Irish Catholic Immigrants in the Antebellum United States,
South Bend, IN: University of Notre Dame Press, 1996.

THINK ABOUT THIS:

What words or images in the song carry political meanings?

A Norwegian Settler
Writes from the Frontier

Some emigrants left their homelands to escape poverty, political oppression, or war. Many of those who immigrated to America's western states and territories, far from the cities, came in search of land that they could own and farm. Occasionally these western settlers found themselves involved in a new kind of war—the final stages of the frontier conflict that had been simmering and flaring between settlers and Native Americans for more than two centuries. In 1866, a pioneer

Norwegian immigrant Beret Olesdater Hagebak and her sod house in Minnesota, around 1896. Many settlers on the western frontier were immigrants, including some women homesteaders.

immigrant wrote from Minnesota to her mother and daughter in Norway, telling how that conflict had affected her.

I DO NOT SEEM TO HAVE BEEN ABLE TO DO so much to write to you, because during the time when the savages raged so fearfully here I was not able to think about anything except being murdered, with my whole family, by these terrible heathen. But God be praised, I escaped with my life, unharmed by them, and my four daughters also came through the danger unscathed.

Guri and Britha were carried off by the wild Indians, but they got a chance the next day to make their escape. . . . I myself wandered aimlessly around on my land with my youngest daughter, and I had to look on while they shot my precious husband dead, and in my sight my dear son Ole was shot through the shoulder. . . . We also found my oldest son Endre shot dead. . . . To be an eye-witness to these things and to see many others wounded and killed was almost too much for a poor woman; but God be thanked, I kept my life and my sanity, though all my movable property was torn away and stolen. . . .

"To be an eye-witness to these things and to see many others wounded and killed was almost too much for a poor woman."

I must also let you know that my daughter Gjaertru has land, which they received from the government under a law that has been passed, called in our language "the Homestead law," . . . and after they have lived there five years they receive a deed and complete possession of the property and can sell it if they want to or keep it if they want to. She lives about twenty-four American miles from here and is doing well. . . .

. . . [I]f you, my dear daughter, would come here, you could buy [my land], and then it would not be necessary to let it fall into the hands of strangers.

—Guri Endreden, letter, in Theodore C. Blegen, "Immigrant Women and the American Frontier," Norwegian-American Studies, vol. 5, 1930.

THINK ABOUT THIS:

1. Can you think of reasons why the Indians might have attacked the Norwegian immigrants?

2. If you were the daughter addressed in the last paragraph, would you be interested in going to America and buying your mother's land?

"Liberty Only through Force": George Engel of the Chicago Eight

Some immigrants felt that the United States, while better than the countries they had left, was not perfect. In the late nineteenth and early twentieth centuries, immigrant workers made great contributions to the labor, reform, and progressive movements, which worked to improve conditions for workers, slum dwellers, and the poor. Some immigrants adopted socialism, the theory that the government, not wealthy individuals, should own resources and manufacturing plants. And some, seeing the great gap between rich and poor, powerful and powerless, voiced the ideas of anarchism, which called for the tearing down of existing political, social, and economic orders, in the hope that a more just society, with equal distribution of wealth, would somehow take their place. In 1886, during a scuffle between anarchist demonstrators and police in Haymarket Square

The 1886 riot in Haymarket Square roused fears among some Americans that immigrants were politically dangerous.

in Chicago, someone threw a bomb, killing seven policemen. Eight of the demonstrators were arrested. None, however, was accused of actually throwing the bomb. Instead, they were tried for spreading the ideas that had inspired the unknown bomb thrower. Seven were condemned to death, one to a prison term. Each had a chance to present a statement to the court.

WHEN, IN THE YEAR 1872, I left Germany because it had become impossible for me to gain there, by the labor of my hands, a livelihood such as man is worthy to enjoy—the introduction of machinery having ruined the smaller craftsmen and made the outlook for the future appear very dark to them—I concluded to fare with my family to the land of America, the land that had been praised to me by so many as the land of liberty. On the occasion of my arrival at Philadelphia, on the 8th of January, 1873, my heart swelled with joy in the hope and in the belief that in the future I would live among free men, and in a free country. I made up my mind to become a good citizen of this country, and congratulated myself on having left Germany, and landed in this glorious republic. And I believe my past history will bear witness that I have ever striven to be a good citizen of this country. This is the first occasion of my standing before an American court, and on this occasion it is murder of which I am accused. And for what reason do I stand here? For what reasons am I accused of murder? The same that caused me to leave Germany—the poverty—the misery of the working classes.

And here, too, in this "free republic," in the richest country of the world, there are numerous proletarians for whom no table is set; who, as outcasts of society, stray joylessly through life. I have seen human beings gather their daily food from the garbage heaps of the streets, to quiet therewith their knawing hunger.

"I have seen human beings gather their daily food from the garbage heaps of the streets."

knawing
gnawing

. . . We see from the history of this country that the first colonists won their liberty only through force; that through force slavery was abolished, and just as the man who agitated against slavery in this country, had to ascend the gallows, so also must we. He who speaks for the workingman today must hang.

—*From "Address of George Engel,"* The Accused and the Accusers: The Famous Speeches of the Eight Chicago Anarchists in Court, *Chicago: Socialistic Publishing Co., n.d.*

1. How do you think Engel would define *freedom*?

2. To what past movements does Engel compare his own political action? Do you agree with his position?

Golden Dreams, Ragged Reality: Rocco Corresca Remembers His *Padrone*

Not all immigrants were generous and helpful toward their fellow countrymen and countrywomen. Once they had gotten a foothold in the United States and learned their way around, some immigrants took advantage of the less experienced. In 1902 a young immigrant from Naples, Italy, described his relationship with Bartolo, his *padrone* (patron or protector and boss).

NOW AND THEN I HAD HEARD THINGS about America—that it was a far-off country where everybody was rich and that Italians went there and made plenty of money, so that they could return to Italy and live in pleasure ever after. One day I met a young man who pulled out a handful of gold and told me he had made that in America in a few days.

"One day I met a young man who pulled out a handful of gold and told me he had made that in America in a few days."

. . . We came to Brooklyn to a wooden house . . . full of Italians from Naples. Bartolo had a room on the third floor and there were fifteen men in the room, all boarding with Bartolo. . . .

Journalist and social reformer Jacob Riis took this photograph of immigrant men in a New York tenement. It appeared in his 1890 book *How the Other Half Lives*, which documented conditions in America's urban slums.

Bartolo told us to go out and pick rags and get bottles. He gave us bags and hooks and showed us the ash barrels. On the streets where the fine houses are the people . . . put out good things, like mattresses and umbrellas. . . . We brought all these to Bartolo and he made them new and sold them again on the sidewalk; but mostly we brought rags and bones. . . . Most of the men in our room worked at digging the sewer. Bartolo got them the work and they paid him about one quarter of their wages. Then he charged them for board and he bought the clothes for them, too. . . . [Bartolo] . . . is now a very rich man. The men that were living with him had just come to the country and could not speak English. . . . Bartolo told us all that we must work for him and that if we did not the police would come and put us in prison.

He gave us very little money, and our clothes were some of those that we had found in the street. Still we had enough to eat and we had meat quite often, which we never had in Italy.

—Rocco Corresca, in "The Biography of a Bootblack," Independent 54, December 4, 1902.

THINK ABOUT THIS:

1. How can you tell that Bartolo's treatment of the immigrants was unfair?

2. What would you do in Corresca's circumstances?

A Danish Immigrant's American Saga

Carl Christian Jensen came to the United States from Denmark in 1906. Years later he wrote *An American Saga*, in which he describes some of the challenges of starting life over in a new land—including the challenge of learning to talk all over again in a new language.

"I had to learn life over in a brand-new world."

I WAS A MAN AND STRONGER than most men. Yet my second childhood began the day I entered my new country. I had to learn life over in a brand-new world. And I could not talk. My first desire was for chocolate drops, and I pointed my finger at them. My second was for fishing tackle, and I pointed my finger at a wrapped cord and heaved up an imaginary fish. I used baby talk. "Price?" I asked. And later in the day, "Vatsprice?" Saleswomen answered me with motherly grimaces.

I never quite got over my second childhood. I doubt that any immigrant does—with his hasty, often harsh attuning to the new world.

—Carl Christian Jensen, An American Saga, *Boston: Little, Brown and Company, 1927.*

Think about This:

1. Why do you think Jensen felt like a child again when he arrived in the United States?
2. What words or images does he use to support the theme of a "second childhood"?

Schoolchildren in New York City's Lower East Side start the day
with a salute to the flag, learning to become loyal citizens.

Chapter 7

Becoming American

SOME IMMIGRANTS CAME TO AMERICA not to stay but merely to work for a while so that they could return to better lives in their countries of origin. The rate of return varied from time to time, depending upon whether economic conditions in the United States were favorable to the immigrants or not. It also varied among ethnic groups—Scandinavian immigrants, for example, seldom returned to their homelands, but large numbers of Chinese, British, Irish, and Italian immigrants did so. Still, the majority of those who immigrated to the United States came to stay.

Most mastered the immediate challenges of finding housing and work. Those who didn't speak English either learned some English or used sign language or interpreters to communicate. In many immigrant families, children became the natural interpreters. If they were young when they arrived in the United States, they soon learned English by playing with other kids or in school. Children born in the United States often grew up speaking two languages. At school or in public places they spoke English, while at home they and their parents talked in the language of the old country.

Children raised questions of identity for some immigrants. People who came to America felt two conflicting desires. On one hand, many immigrants strongly wanted to assimilate, which meant to become part of mainstream American culture and society—to be regarded as Americans, not foreigners. If they couldn't completely make the transition, they hoped that their children could. But many immigrants, on the other hand, feared losing their cultural heritage. They saw how easy it was to slip out of touch

Children of poor Jewish immigrants in New York City study the Hebrew scriptures, around 1900. Through private schools, social organizations, and festivals, immigrants strove to maintain their traditions.

with family and friends they had left behind, and they wondered whether they were leaving behind other things as well: languages, customs, religious practices. They founded ethnic cultural organizations and schools to preserve these traditions and pass them on to younger generations. Battle lines were often drawn in immigrant households between parents who feared that their children or grandchildren were becoming too American and young people who were impatient with extra language classes and Old World customs.

In the end, each immigrant decided for himself or herself what being American meant. Today the children and grandchildren and great-grandchildren of those who came during the century of immigration, as well as the new immigrants still arriving, continue to seek a balance between blending in and maintaining an ethnic identity. By doing both, immigrants past and present have made American society unique.

The First German-American Senator: Carl Schurz Enters Politics

As a twenty-year-old student, Carl Schurz took part in a revolutionary movement that tried to bring republican government to his native Germany in 1848–1849. The movement failed, and many of the idealistic revolutionaries, including Schurz, emigrated to the United States to escape punishment. Schurz became a lawyer and a supporter of Abraham Lincoln and the Republican Party which formed to get Lincoln elected to the presidency. He fought on the Union side in the Civil War, reaching the rank of major general.

After the war Schurz settled in Missouri. In 1869 his fellow citizens elected him to the U.S. Senate, where he remained for six years. He then held the cabinet post of secretary of the interior from 1877 to 1881. Schurz, the first German American to serve his adopted country as senator and cabinet member, wrote about his life. The first of these passages describes a speech Schurz made about democracy in Boston in 1859. The second tells of his emotions on taking his Senate seat.

THE OLD-FASHIONED HALL WAS FILLED with a typical Boston audience. Here I was to strike my blow at Nativism and the politics of sly tricks and petty scheming. My speech seemed to have a good effect. I spoke with great passion and mainly emphasized the concept which was my guiding principle throughout my entire political career in America: the important part which this republic has to play in the progress of humanity toward democratic forms of government, and the resulting enormous responsibility of the American people to the entire civilized world. It may sound unlikely and almost ridiculously presumptuous to assert that foreign-born Americans can be more impassioned and sincere in their patriotism for America than many native-born ones are, and yet my experience showed that to be the case.

"Only a little more than sixteen years had passed since I landed in America as a homeless refugee."

I clearly remember my feelings upon taking my seat: I was all choked up. I had attained the highest public office I could ever have dreamed of. I was still young; I had just turned forty. Only a little more than sixteen years had passed since

Carl Schurz fled the "shipwreck of the revolutionary movement in Europe" to become the first German-American senator and cabinet member in the United States.

I landed in America as a homeless refugee, rescued from the great shipwreck of the revolutionary movement in Europe. At that time the American people took me in with heartwarming hospitality; they opened all the many promising opportunities the New World had to offer, as generously to me as to their native children. And now I was a member of the highest legislative body of the greatest Republic. Would I ever be able to repay my debt of gratitude to this country and justify all the honors heaped upon me?

—*Rüdiger Werisch, editor,* Carl Schurz, Revolutionary and Statesman: His Life in Personal and Official Documents, with Illustrations, *Munich: Heinz Moos Verlag, 1979.*

THINK ABOUT THIS:

1. Why might Schurz have felt that foreign-born Americans were often more passionately patriotic than native-born ones?
2. Do you think that an immigrant from China would have been met with the same "heartwarming hospitality" and "promising opportunities" as Schurz?

"Be Worthy": Advice for Immigrants

In 1908 the Bureau of Immigration and Naturalization, the federal office in charge of immigration at that time, issued a booklet called *Information for Immigrants Concerning the United States: Its Opportunities, Government, and Institutions.* The booklet provided answers to seven questions asked by "most of those who come to the United States." Among the questions were, "Is it or is it not true that anyone can become rich in this country?" and "What is the religion of this country?" The booklet was prepared by the National Society of the Sons of the American Revolution, an organization of men who could trace their ancestry to someone who had fought in the Revolutionary War (1775–1783). A portion of the booklet's text follows.

THE PERSON WHO LEAVES THE LAND in which he was born, and goes to another to make his home, wants to know the truth about a number of things in the land to which he goes.

To give such information this is prepared, not by any set of men who are interested in availing themselves of your labor or seeking to get your money, but by a society which has for its object the teaching to all of a love of country, and is composed of the descendants of the men to whom the United States owes its existence as a distinct country. . . .

"This is a great country to which you have come."

This is a great country to which you have come. It extends from where the snow and ice never entirely melt on the north to where frost is never known on the south, from an ocean in the east 3,000 miles to an ocean on the west. It has great lakes and rivers, high mountains, fertile plains and valleys. There are great stores of coal, iron, and natural oil. Almost every variety of fruits and grains is found in large quantities, and great mills and factories manufacture everything that is necessary for comfort. This is the land to which you have come. May you be worthy of it.

—Information for Immigrants Concerning the United States: Its Opportunities, Government, and Institutions, *Washington, DC: Government Printing Office, 1908.*

THINK ABOUT THIS:

1. How do the booklet's authors set themselves apart from other sources of information? Why do you think they do so?
2. When the authors ask immigrants to "be worthy" of their new home, what do you think they mean?

A Bulgarian Immigrant Makes a Decision

Life in ethnic colonies, surrounded by people with a shared background and shared memories of the old country, was safe and comforting for many immigrants troubled by the sense of being strangers in a strange land. Stoyan Christowe, however, rejected such a life. He came to the United States from the eastern European nation of Bulgaria in 1911 and spent several years living in a Bulgarian neighborhood in an eastern city. Then he went to Montana and studied English—an experience that gave him a new vision of his future in America.

THE LANGUAGE WAS FULL OF MYSTERIES AND ADVENTURE. Every new word I learned brought to me something new and exciting. Since my contact with America and its people was necessarily limited, through the language I sought to link myself with them. If I mastered the speech, I felt certain I would come nearer attaining my American ideal. I knew then as I know now that the language was the passport to my America.

The track hands who came to Montana for the summers and returned East for the winters to live in colonies made up of their own countrymen had little in common with America. Many had been in America ten years and still they were strangers in this country. They thought old-country thoughts, spoke only their native tongues. All of them were interested in making money, and that was their only contact with America. I was fortunate to see the tragedy of these people. And I did not want the same thing to happen to me.

I was now, after five years, on the eve of a second journey to America. I was ready and eager to return to the East, but not to the colony. America was not there. My America was elsewhere. No train or steamship could take me to it. I alone must find it.

"I knew then as I know now that the language was the passport to my America."

—Stoyan Christowe, This Is My Country, *1938, quoted in*
Frances Cavanah, *editor,* We Came to America: An Anthology,
Philadelphia: Macrae Smith Co., 1954.

1. Christowe speaks of making "a second voyage to America." What does he mean?
2. Why does Christowe describe the situation of the immigrant workers he saw as a "tragedy"?

Ernesto Galarza: "The Americanization of Mexican Me"

Ernesto Galarza was born in 1905 in the town of Jalcocotàn, Mexico. His family immigrated to California when he was eight years old, and at once he was plunged into school with American-born children as well as other young immigrants, from Japan, Italy, Portugal, Korea, and Yugoslavia. Years later he described his childhood in *Barrio Boy,* a book about growing up in a Hispanic community within an American city. It describes his elementary school and the educator whose task was "the Americanization of Mexican me."

MISS HOPLEY AND HER TEACHERS NEVER LET US FORGET why we were at Lincoln: for those who were alien, to become good Americans; for those who were so born, to accept the rest of us. . . . The school was not so much a melting-pot as a griddle where Miss Hopley and her helpers warmed knowledge into us and roasted racial hatreds out of us.

At Lincoln, making us into Americans did not mean scrubbing away what made us originally foreign. The teachers called us as our parents did, or as close as they could pronounce our names in Spanish or Japanese. No one was ever scolded or punished for speaking in his native tongue on the playground. Matti told the class about his mother's down quilt, which she had made in Italy with the fine feathers of a thousand geese. Encarnación acted out how boys learned to fish in the Philippines. I astounded the third grade with the story of my travels on a stagecoach, which nobody else in the class had seen except in the museum at Sutter's Fort. After a visit to the Crocker Art Gallery and its collection of heroic paintings of the golden age of California, someone showed a silk scroll with a Chinese painting. Miss Hopley herself had a way of expressing wonder over these matters before a class, her eyes wide open until they popped slightly. It was easy for me to feel that becoming a proud American, as she said we should, did not mean feeling ashamed of being a Mexican.

—*Ernesto Galarza,* Barrio Boy, *South Bend, IN: University of Notre Dame Press, 1971.*

Think about This:

1. Do you think that Miss Hopley's approach to educating multicultural children was the standard for her day?
2. How does young Ernesto's experience of school compare with your own?

A Note on the Principle of "Americanization"

In the early years of the twentieth century, a New York City publishing company produced a series of books called Americanization Studies. Each book dealt with a different aspect of immigrant life in the United States. The publishers added a note to each volume that explained the principle of "Americanization" upon which the series was based.

. . . AMERICANIZATION IN THIS STUDY HAS BEEN considered as the union of native and foreign born in all the most fundamental relationships and activities of our national life. For Americanization is the uniting of new with native-born Americans in fuller common understanding and appreciation to secure by means of self-government the highest welfare of all. Such Americanization should perpetuate no unchangeable political, domestic, and economic regime delivered once for all to the fathers, but a growing and broadening of national life, inclusive of the best wherever found. With all our rich heritages, Americanism will develop best through a mutual giving and taking of contributions from both newer and older Americans in the interest of the commonweal. This study has followed such an understanding of Americanization.

—*Kate Holladay Claghorn*, The Immigrant's Day in Court,
New York: Harper & Brothers, 1923.

THINK ABOUT THIS:

1. How does this view of immigration compare with that of Israel Zangwill in *The Melting-Pot*?
2. If you were a new immigrant, how would you feel about this definition of *Americanization*?

Preserving the Immigrant Heritage: Akemi Kikumura

During the second half of the twentieth century, immigrant studies became a recognized field of research. Historians examined the causes and effects of the century of immigration. Scholars collected and published old interviews and letters that shone light on the lives and experiences of immigrants, and some immigrants wrote their own stories. One scholar, Akemi Kikumura, wanted to investigate

Japanese emigrants on their way to Hawaii in 1904 receive vaccinations. Many Asian-American families came to the United States by way of Hawaii, which needed workers for its plantations of sugarcane and pineapples.

the lives of Japanese women who had come to the United States early in the century. She told the story of one such woman in *Through Harsh Winters: The Life of a Japanese Immigrant Woman*. Kikumura explained, "This book was written out of respect and admiration for these courageous women who had managed to transform hardship, suffering, and despair into determination, understanding, and hope. In an attempt to capture their spirit and learn more about my own cultural heritage, I had decided to write a life history of my mother, using her own words (as I translated them) to tell a story about an issei woman's experience in America." In writing about one immigrant's life, Kikumura explored her family history. Here, her mother describes how she persuaded her husband, Kikumura's father, to come to America.

issei
immigrant from Japan; first-generation Japanese American

I KEPT COAXING PAPA, "Let's go to America." I was on the adventurous side. I wasn't afraid of anything. I wanted to see foreign countries and besides I had consented to marriage with Papa because I had the dream of seeing America. I didn't care for him much . . . he didn't have much education. I could have married a real good person in Japan, but I wanted to see America and Papa was a way to get there.

"I kept coaxing Papa, 'Let's go to America.'"

Grandfather Tanaka said to us, "You have this much—mountains, means— America is not such a good place and besides you may never be able to get back, so don't go." My mother wasn't happy that we were leaving, either. She said, if we stayed, she would give us the noodle shop that she had purchased and we could run it together.

But I kept urging Papa, "Let's go to America." I just couldn't wait to see it. We decided to go for a short while, make enough money for our trip, then return home. With that thought in mind, we borrowed $350 from Grandfather Tanaka and $150 from my parents and we left Yokohama on the *Korea Maru,* bound for America. It was January, 1923.

—*Akemi Kikumura,* Through Harsh Winters: The Life of a Japanese Immigrant Woman, *Novato, CA: Chandler & Sharp, 1981.*

THINK ABOUT THIS:

1. How would you describe Kikumura's mother?
2. Are there immigrants in your family or among your family friends? Do you know their stories?

Time Line

1790 U.S. Congress passes first national immigration law, the Naturalization Act, which allows a "free white person" to become a citizen after two years in the country

1819 First U.S. Passenger Act limits number of passengers on ships arriving in United States

1700s

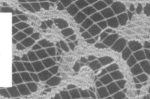

1820 Federal government starts keeping immigration records

1803 British Passenger Act reduces immigration from Great Britain; Louisiana Purchase doubles size of United States and opens land to European immigrants